Winter in June

Lorette C. Luzajic

Mixed Up Media Editions
2021

Winter in June
copyright Lorette C. Luzajic 2021
Mixed Up Media Editions.
all rights reserved.
ISBN 9798507886036
www.mixedupmedia.ca

On *Pretty Time Machine*

"'Everyone is looking for moments like these, small, frail, beautiful connections where the world stops for just a second.' ('The Phenomenal World'). These bittersweet, lyrical, yet often eviscerating poems are ekphrastic explorations that examine life's fragile connections with ruthless intent. Sparing no one, Luzajic strips the shiny façade from her subjects, exposing their humanness, and her own." *Alexis Rhone Fancher,* author of *The Dead Kid Poems,* poetry editor, *Cultural Weekly*

"Astonishing, urgent, leaves nothing behind. Each brief narrative emboldens an emotional truth with language that is fierce, elegant, and unflinching; Luzajic's writing is nothing short of brilliant." *Karen Schauber,* editor, *The Group of Seven Reimagined: Contemporary Stories Inspired by Historic Canadian Paintings*

"Best writing I've read by a living writer since who knows when." Darrell Epp, author of *After Hours, Sinners Dance, Imaginary Maps*

"This book's more honest than you. It'll hold your hand and bring you places." *Noah Wareness,* author of *Meatheads, Real is the Word They Use to Contain Us*

On Other Works

"This girl was born to write, and she writes as well as I do." *Crad Kilodney,* author of *Putrid Scum, Shakespeare for White Trash, Girl on the Subway*

"Luzajic, like Wonder Woman, is her own institution." *Paul Robinson,* Blog Critics

"All around creative genius...Lorette, you are a superstar." *Ariel Gore,* author of *How to Become a Famous Writer Before You're Dead,* and *The End of Eve*

"Imaginative, witty...surprising, profound, very human, touching, sassy." *Thomas Moore*, bestselling author of *Care of the Soul*

Table of Contents

1 The Last Time I Showed Up at Midnight
2 Blood
3 The Boys of Summer
4 The Chechia Makers
5 Mizuko Kuyo
6 The Portrait Artist
7 Snow Tangerines
9 Still Alive
10 Homecoming
11 Billy, Don't Lose My Number
13 The Dead Bird House
14 The Crying Room
15 Benedict and the Pomelo
16 The Red Van
18 Dandy Warhol
21 The Thief
22 The YouTube Years
23 The Phantom of Flatwoods
26 A Truckload of Apples
27 Charlie's Angel
28 Blindness
31 Stutter
32 Karen and Karen
34 Tightrope Love
35 November Woods
36 Kitten Heels
38 The Garden
40 Darker
41 The Nightingale

42 First Bluegrass Lesson
43 Lepidoptera
46 Bull
47 Day of the Dead
48 Cages
49 The Gandy Dark
50 A Parable of the Blind Leading the Blind
53 Lucky Peace
54 Cuda
58 Found Objects
59 Havoc
60 Barn
61 Ruby Slippers
63 Cliff Hanger
64 Death in Tepito
66 The Hell Cat
68 Pho
70 Running Hot and Cold: Variations
73 Promiscuity
75 Online Quarantine Curiosity Cabinet, Amazon Edition
77 Night Swimming
78 Pulp Fiction
79 Mrs. Jones
80 Triskaidekaphobia
82 Jalapenos
85 Tiny Dancer
86 Checkers
87 Outlaw Shit
91 Hebe
92 The Keychain Monkeys
94 Night Sax in Mexico City

95 The Paper Dark
97 Tower of Horses
98 The Shawarma King
99 White
100 The Peanut Butter Yarmulke
102 Simon Says
104 Salt
105 The Nowhere Man
106 The Land of Wind and Ghosts
109 Soppressata
110 Sunday Bloody Sunday
112 Rapture
113 The Wishing Machine
115 The White Room
116 Sweet and Sour
117 Twitter
118 Horoscope
119 I Hope You Are Wrong
121 Wild Things
127 Fifteen Shades of Gray
128 Disco Nefertiti
129 Mr. Jones
130 The Neon Raven
134 Rocket Man
135 Our Daily Bread
136 The Narcissists
138 The Mists of Catalan
139 Downpour
140 The Pink Cafe
141 Night Flight
142 Feeling the Blues

143 Drowned World
144 Yahtzee
147 Conceal/Carry
148 Robin Eggs
149 Eternity and Impermanence
150 Girl at the Market
151 Quill and Quire
152 The Passenger
153 Ventriloquy
154 Green Fan, Sleeping Lady
155 A Wrinkle in Time
156 Kneeling
157 American Psycho
158 The Nowhere Train
161 Connective Tissue
162 The Skeleton Flower
163 Winter in June

Readers can view the ekphrastic inspirations or follow along with the artworks at www.mixedupmedia.ca/winter-in-june.html.

for Moshy
the *sweetiest* thing that I ever did see

"In the end, we'll all become stories."
Margaret Atwood

The Last Time I Showed Up at Midnight

after *The Last Time I Showed Up at Midnight,* Lorette C. Luzajic (Canada) 2014

The last time I showed up at midnight, you had blown out all the candles and the only sound in the smoke was the laboured humming and tumble of the ice machine. The whisky was open but pushed aside. I tipped some into an espresso cup and took my medicine. The humidity had an aura of its own, pressing the small of my back and my neck like an intense and patient lover. I fumbled for ice but only thin shells fell to my hands. There was a low pulse of jazz, so faint I knew it was the ghost of last night's music gone. The stars were almost wiped invisible by the saltwater in the air, but I could still see a few blinking faintly and far. I thought about leaving a note before I disappeared forever, but I knew you'd know I'd been there.

Blood

after *Two Sisters,* Theodore Chasseriau (France) 1843

The sisters, light and dark, rain and shine. Corene, blunt cut burnt sienna and poems about midnight. Dawn, wavy and feathered, as blonde and buoyant as the day's first glow. The scent of cinnamon and oranges. Corene would wander into the woods for solitude, spend all of Saturday in the library to avoid birthday parties and team sports. Dawn was a magnet, a hub, warm, loved everyone, stacked up a few dozen Valentines every winter. One sister does gold highlights, pastel blouses, a quick peach gloss over lids and mouth. The other has lips like a cardinal and holes everywhere for hardware. Dawn is married to her teenage sweetheart, takes her three flaxen-tressed boys to a big box church with drums and hands lifted in the air. Corene was an atheist for a long time, and is usually still wasted on Sunday mornings. She has no children and her husband is dead. Today Dawn is flipping flapjacks for a choir. Still in capri pajamas. Corene rinses the blueberries, slices up bananas. Dawn does not understand her sister's paintings, but even so, her room is covered in them. Corene does not get new country, but she is bobbing along to the heartache as she drizzles the pancakes in nutmeg and maple. It was an impossible promise, to never be divided, but they have kept it since tweenage pinkie swear. They are refuge and sanctuary. *You'll never be friends,* Mother used to say, in that trademark singsong taunt of hers, *because your Father's traitor juice runs through your veins.* And they both saw right through it then and there, knew that his blood was the glue.

The Boys of Summer

after *Car Wash,* William Wray (USA) contemporary

It was a one trick town, I told you, but you shrugged, said you'd been tricked before. Let your wheels spin dust at the edge of the lot where you waited for me. I was world weary already, even though I'd never left. Slipped in shotgun with an armload of popsicles and a jug of Domaine D'Or. Wondered if you'd kiss me or grope at my thigh. Once I booked an appointment with the school shrink, cried, asked her if anyone would ever touch me. She said, one day you'll think about this meeting and laugh, you'll have had so many lovers. I didn't think the years would go by, that I would blink and be fifty. No one does. After school I would vacuum my grandmother's room for a five spot, then sit at her swollen feet with a plate of stale cookies and listen to her lamentations. The summer was almost gone and you hadn't yet made a move. I doused myself in Love's Baby Soft, showed up with hash in hopes of hurrying things along. You didn't bite, and I was worried. *You think you won't find love,* Oma said once, pushing her ivory brush through long and oily silver tresses. *But the real story is how it is so fleeting.*

The Chechia Makers

after *The Merchant,* Giulio Rosati (Italy) by 1917

On my morning stroll through the walled city, I meet the fez makers of Tunis in the souk. The shop is green and folksy, more a cupboard than a store, and an old-timer at a sort of sewing machine beckons me in. He shares a lengthy history, complete with vintage photographs from his grandfather and the National Geographic. He takes my hand and runs it across the thick shorn wool he's spinning. The red chechia makers are beating the dead horse of a dying art, and when I leave, empty handed, the merchant is crushed. I can feel centuries wedged between us. The medinas of Tunisia were relentless- those old-world sales tactics could really put a female traveller on edge. I was stalked, followed, blockaded, and bullied, if men's first friendly charms failed to sell a trinket. I'd been sold stuff with ferocity in Mexico and Jerusalem, but this was different altogether. It left me wary and vigilant, ready to run. One stalked me for two hours, sitting himself at the café I escaped to, mocking me and my assumed wealth and shoving photos of his children under my coffee cup with his iPhone. He used his arms to block me from the exit of the city, right at the gate of my motel. I was almost afraid. That was the taste in my mouth that made me rush out of the shop without a fez. If I could turn back now, I would buy the damn hat. It was simple and beautiful. I can still see the old man's nubby fingertips, his twisted knuckles, strong and sensual against the needles and the spools. The ancient cap makers survived the new millennium. Before the next century turns, they will be ghosts.

Mizuko Kuyo

after Mizuko Kuyo gardens, Japan

for Rebecca

1. My water baby: tiny golden feet, each toe a plump raisin. This is what I have lost: the future I made, that fate chose to deny me.

2. I named her. *Judith.* It came to me when I held her cold form against my tired breasts, just for a moment.

3. Years later, visiting Japan, I add a jizo statue to the garden of lost children. In the silence, the sound of heaven pulling down.

The Portrait Artist

Nude in the Mirror, Marie Laurencin (France) 1916

All of the artist's black-haired beauties look just like her. She convinces you that she wears big floppy bows, ruffles piled high on hats and a swan's neck. That her pupils are dark saucers staining the whole of her eyes. Happiness is a paint-splotch dove and a blue lap dog. Wisdom is a lute, a mirror, an open book.

Snow Tangerines

after *Untitled (White, Orange, and Yellow)* Mark Rothko (USA, b. Latvia) 1953

You are surrounded by spindly stilettos, fit to flit on stilts-y legs, women in pricy and papery little dresses. Thoroughbreds, Miko called them once, his face just an inch from his canvas, scrutinizing flecks of white and pale peach paint. Miko could make mountains out of a smudge of orange and sometimes he liked to mix the pigment right there in the palm of his hand. Said it felt elemental. You loved that, how he always touched everything, every window, every door, every utensil, everything he browsed when shopping, every Mourvèdre, every sweater, every clementine. Your bookshelves have his finger trails across their topography, and every ornament and tea miniature in your clutter bears his DNA.

Now they are here to see him, the horses, and they shift and flutter with nervous electricity and something more vicious, something hungry. They don't see you. They don't see you at all. Their eyes sweep right past your paintings in search of his. They don't see your cruel and precise wedges of winter, the impasto of frost and silver.

But so? Your work speaks for itself, to those paying attention. Look, Miko is saying, with both of his hands right up against the texture of your painting. He wags against a lacquered nail fast approaching: only he can touch you. See here? he says. See how the world stops inside her frame, how you are frozen in a dream. You love how Miko sees you and sees right through you. Your oldest friend. There are tangles of rich and ready mares juggling Carmenere and Instagram, and still he only sees what you see, the red wheelbarrow, the spill of tangerines in the snow.

Still Alive

after Clara Peeters

Morning brings small rain, and a small miracle: no line for entry at the Prado. There is a lull in the motion, and we venture into hallowed halls to see Giacometti's skinny shadows. They are spindly critters that mimic our mannerisms as if we are somnambulists feeling our way frantically from room to room. We are sterile before Bosch, chaste before the other Mona Lisa, made gory by Goya's grotesque black dreams. All is still until the still life, the hungry portent of want and need, the offering of fowl and sweetbreads. The saline grit of fish and of olives, earthy and generous, oval, and oily. Clarets of grenadine and red roses.

Homecoming

after *Eight Hearts,* Jim Dine (USA) 1970

Maybe you can feel me pulling away, and that's why you reach for me with some of the longing we started with. I'm not sure where I'm going, or trying to go, because I'm not really going anywhere at all. I'm already home. There's a restlessness that's always with me. There's a sliver of sickness at my centre that might never go away, that thing that makes me run from everything that's good for me. We all have those things, of course, the one we let slip through our fingers, the dream come true we didn't show up for, the last chance to see someone and we just couldn't be bothered, the lost chance we had to make things right but didn't believe until it was too late. You find me sitting in the window under a round slice of moon, watching the rooftops. I tell you I'm not sleepy. I still have these spells, smaller than before, but still, they come over me. *Moments where I feel like I'm dead.* I open the window wider, try to get the night into my veins. You only shrug, put your hand on my heart, tell me it's still beating.

Billy, Don't Lose My Number

after *Aprés-Midi,* Hughie Lee-Smith (USA) 1987

for Billy

Billy comes out of the basement, and his eyes are sore from the sudden light. I ask if he's okay to drive, and he rolls his eyes until they nearly disappear. *I'm just tired, Miss Lorette*, he says. *The night shift can really mess you up.* That's as close to complaining as Billy would ever get, just stating the facts. When a factory chemical spill stripped the skin off his inside arm, before it grew back as ropes and knots, he slathered his seething wrists in aloe and Saran Wrap and clocked in as usual. Billy stayed the night only once, after leaving his debit card in a nearby ATM with no way to get back to the burbs. I pulled out the cheap pleather sofa bed and the cat immediately hopped up on it and splayed himself across the duvet. I loved seeing Billy laugh like that, to have a body to love beside him. It had been years, forever. In the morning, I was going to make him pancakes with cinnamon and bananas but he was gone and it was months before he answered his phone again. Now we speed along the lakeshore, black and white, fat and skinny, and still like siblings of sorts. We see the families spreading picnics along the water's edge, watch shirtless brown boys bumping volley balls over nets beside the highway. Billy smiles, because he thought I'd never find a boyfriend. I cry because I hope he finds a girl who will treat him the way I would treat him if it was up to me. The sun falls into Etobicoke as we slurp our way through the fructose sludge of iced cappuccinos. Billy will go back inside, hibernate through winter even though it's only June. I will call for him in December. For now, I reach across the gear shift for his pointy fingers. He holds my secrets as if they were glass, and I hold his, too, sad and soft as dandelion seeds, weightless as they tumble over the waves.

The Dead Bird House

after *Church Painting,* Stephen Mathews (USA) 2020

We followed the long sky for hours. We were the only ones on the road. The white cotton bolls blooming beneath blue like a mirage. We passed a crooked little church, covered in spray-on prophecies. Tagged, jagged, bedraggled, so many ghosts in the dagger branches. The dead went with me everywhere, no matter where I was going. I did everything I could to make sure no one I loved felt they had to compete with those who had no fight left in them. But when you bury everything before now, you long for what's long gone. It was there at the back of my mind every time the sun started setting on the bay. The shadows descended through the pines along the cove just before we landed home. There were always scattered starlings on that lawn with so many birdhouses tangled in the trees. Why that was so was a mystery. I cast my bets on the obvious: *poison.* I was sure the old hermit who lived there was a sadist. But you said fate took its own turns. That it was possible the dead birds preceded the occupant and that they scared her, too. It was a generous view of her life and people's pasts in general, and I took it. Said maybe you were right and left it there. But inside, I knew the thing wasn't outside of me, it was something coiled tightly within, this darkness that drew death to me. I didn't say it of course. I wanted something else to be true and real, to give you only the thing I had always wished about myself. I wanted to be easy to love.

The Crying Room

after *Hansel in Cage, with Gretel and Witch,* Philip Grot Johann (Germany) by 1892

It has always been that way, since you were small and before you had unfolded. You could have been anybody, and whoever that was and would be was all I'd ever wanted. I read you my own poems and all the ones I found in tattered leather from the rare book nooks I was already taking shelter in. I watched our mother's white belly rise and fall, with you protruding in her sleeping heaving. I wondered what I would say to you when I saw you, but when I did, I wept like a baby and couldn't say anything at all. You wore my face on your face. Well, if there is anything I would do over, it would be to shelter you from her venom and vinegar, but the truth was no one could. Not even Daddy could save us. We were her collateral against him. Thirty two years later, we stood, stooped and shattered in the door frame after our father's funeral. With our sister and her children and all those tiny sandwiches and cakes. Our small tribe, its fallen captain. You gnawed below the quick of your finger, never hiding the grotesque bouquet of stubby digits the way I did in my scarves and my bangles. Let it bleed, you said to me once, when I tried to conceal my lacerated cuticles. Let it bleed, you've earned it.

Benedict and the Pomelo

after *Circus Sideshow,* Georges Seurat (France) 1887

She is ugly, but Benedict loves her best of anyone. The fortune teller is a cascade of tinsel on the grubby linoleum. All dazzle and dangle, all shimmering ribbons and spangles. The jetsam and jangle cannot disguise the oracle's barnacles or hirsute girth: she moves through each room like a gypsy caravan or carnival ship. It was love at first sight in the big tent, where she found him, frantic, fumbling for a lost orange. She saved his act when she pulled a pomelo from her skirts. She almost cracked a smile. He is skinny wiggle to her ample jiggle, tall and striped, a lean tower. Pinched and gaunt against her wide mean glower. She is the sybil, he is the juggler.

The Red Van

after *Standard Station,* Ed Ruscha (USA) 1966

Another mile or two down, there are houses, covered in blinking candy canes or twinkling blue and silver. But here, the only lights in the world are the dim yellow outlines of the petrol pumps on the lot. You stand in blackness, inhaling fumes of winter and gasoline. You are sixteen and miserable: it is Christmas Eve and your shift is only half gone. When another twenty Decembers pass, you will still count this as your favourite job, but there is no way to know this now. You love wearing jeans to work and will never know the hell of fast-food issue polyester slacks. You love being the only girl. You can scratch out song words in Bic pen to your heart's content and smoke anything you want. You can practice your guitar, because no one will hear you save for a few raccoons in the bin out back. There are headlights bobbing now through the trees, and you reach for your hat and mittens. But it is not a customer in need of gasoline, it is the red boss van. Your heart skips the way it always does as you wait to see who is on duty. If it's Jim, fatherly and kind, he will have fresh hot coffee for you from the Donut Diner. Tonight, maybe, a handful of his wife's gingerbread babies, too. But it might be Gareth. If it's Gareth, he will be aloof and polite and distract himself doing a product count or checking on your change. Anything to avoid your eyes, even though you never did tell a soul that he kissed you this past summer. Right here. Even though you wish he would do it again. But tonight he is not looking away. He is looking right at you. His face is uneven and strange. You are about to make a smart remark, ask if Santa missed his stocking, but you say nothing instead. We're closing early, he tells you finally. It's Jim. We found his van this afternoon. He did it to himself. They found Jim. He shakes out a Rothman's King in the sadness between you, offers it to you, pulls another out for himself. Lights them both. He was such a nice man, Gareth says, because it is true, and it is a phrase you will hate forever from now on. You picture Jim's wife, looking up from her baking at the knock of the door, thinking it is carollers or the kids come home early. You wonder how a man's life can just be erased, one moment to the next, no rhyme or reason. It is what you are both thinking while you stand there in that silent night.

Dandy Warhol

after Andy

1. I watch you watch him sleeping. Not for the full film- I am fading to flicker long before your patience gave out on the camera. Possibly the slowest cinema in history. You thought it would be ridiculous to have long movies about nothing, six hours of footage of your friend fast asleep. He might turn or stir but mostly he's just breathing. I hesitate to read too much into it, but can't help wondering if there's something more there after all. As if you wanted to witness the unseen, see what it is we usually sleep through.

2. We have come a long way to find you, Andy. Drove all the way down to Pittsburgh, winding past manicured American churchyards, tidy and quaint gardens with old graves and corny little plaques or statues of the stars and stripes, or big bums.

3. We stop at the outskirts in the kind of grimy little diner of our dreams, order grilled Cheez Whiz on Wonder Bread, and a bowl of steaming tomato soup.

4. Some said you were celibate. That you never had love. That no one ever wanted you in that way.

5. No one, that is, except God. You went to meet him, clandestine, most days, kneeling in a stone cathedral and basking in the beauty. Mass wasn't everything- you wore a scapular, served soup to the homeless at a mission. I picture

you small and naked without your white wig, feigning slumber when I peek in, surrounded by a thousand glow in the dark plastic virgins.

6. Others say you started the whole virgin rumour yourself to make sure people never stopped guessing, or talking.

7. I wander through the warehouse, through the mad-dashed factory of mass manufactured originals, soup tins, daisies, dollar signs, Marilyn, Mickey Mouse, bananas.

8. The greatest paintings on all seven floors of the Andy Warhol museum are the guns. Red and black, black and white, pink and red and white and black. The revolving revolvers. You made them after you took a bullet for all men. It shattered your spleen and you had to keep your innards from spilling out from that day forward. The woman who popped that bullet was a terrorist: she wanted to kill the patriarchy, to eradicate all men. Fey and fizzy, awkward, and eternally bewildered, you were an unlikely target for her scorn. You turned to the second amendment to defend yourself from the accusations at the heart of her attempted murder, brought in your metaphorical big guns, endless wall wide screen-silks outlining her death wish. Grim, but even so, triumphant, in peaceful protest, how you rose from the dead to defy her. Each barrel your giant middle finger.

9. But I love the cats most. Tabby after tabby. Green, red, freckled. Blue and orange. Orange and blue.

10. Your tomb is among a small sprinkle of stones on a sunny hillside at the side of the highway. You have been covered in dahlias, clam chowder, a teddy, and a plastic bottle of holy water.

11. No one knows where to find you. Before we finally get there, we asked a man watering his lawn a block away from where you were at rest. *Who?* he asked. *Andrew Warhol? How do you spell that?*

12. Your city is a thousand bridges, and old gargoyle churches transplanted from Transylvania. Where your kin was knit. Landed before American steel was thrown into the soup. The city of steel, of concrete, cranes, and stained-glass windows.

13. The museum is grand and austere, missing the frantic speedy frenzy of the freaks you found were friends. It all feels like some sort of epic parody, except for the kicker at the core. That you were the real deal, the coolest one among them.

14. How did you do it? How did you command the bold and the beautiful and all their millions? You and your tooth-shorn stubby fingers, your pasty pallor and Einstein wig. You and your golly-whiz gees. You polish your specs on the loose pockets of your polyester slacks, slide them back up to your pale beady blues along a greasy cushion of nose. Golly, oh, really? Oh, Gosh, I don't know, you admit, lisping a little. Sip your Coke and shrug.

The Thief

after *Spanish Curiosity Shop,* William Merritt Chase (USA) 1883

It was all the little trinkets he brought for you, all the things you didn't know you wanted. Each one a surprise you couldn't have guessed. There was the orange blossom water from North Africa, sweet and sunny on your skin, and lapis pigment powder for your paintings. An antique sleigh bell, a dragon of red jade. You learned to make love in the same spirit, curious, sensual, with a wide appreciation for beauty. Saw how real value was in the details, in the magic of a place, or in a mystery. Long after you were happily married to someone else, you ran into a mutual acquaintance, who said your once paramour was still bribing women with stolen baubles. You may have suspected as much then, but even now it doesn't change much for you. He gave you the world and showed you how to look closely. There are different ways to love, you think, different kinds of gifts.

The YouTube Years

after *Cosa Chiedere,* Tommaso Santucci (Italy) contemporary

Just before Cash's mournful, prophetic death carol, a psychedelic ad for fabric softener with a dippy house husband and a dog. Nothing is sacred. You watch Johnny spill his heart and guts for real, for empty, an old man who knows it's time to fold his hands on top of the piano. As the black birds swell over the screen, the scene jumps to just the right golf clubs for summer. The next video shows a dozen thugs piling in on a tween at a bus stop, and after that the news comes at you, blood and bombs and the death of God and all the things that Cash was warning.

The Phantom of Flatwoods

after *Pandemic Evolution, Day 58,* Matthew Wolfe (USA) 2020

The cusp of dusk, and not quite fall. The woods were still warm. Braxton County, West Virginia. Near four hours from the big city, and Fork Mountain just below. The tobacco was almost finished; only four million pounds of it this year.

The brothers had their friend Tommy and a bushel of Golden Delicious in the bed of the blue truck. Flatwoods would soon overflow with pie. Apple, of course, and peach cream. Shoofly, too, pie oozing sticky molasses, attracting every gnat under the sun. Goes down nice with a cold beer, Fred thought. They usually settled for iced tea. It was hard to get your hands on the stuff in this county, and none of them were old enough for whatever it was their uncle made under the moon. Maybe next year.

Ed spun a cigarette from a pouch of Yellow Orinoco, steered with his other hand. Shadows danced in the near dark. He drove slower near the trestle so they could take in the last copper slice of sun. That's when they saw the sky falling into the road ahead of them.

Fred braked. They heard Tommy yelp, felt the staccato thuds of rolling goldens. Jagged fragments of black and silver ice on fire, crashing through the stars and spilling like coins on either side of road.

What was that?!?!? Ed's voice was an octave higher than it had been at the last bend. Tommy frogged over the edge of the truck, scrambled into the cabin. Ed was thinking his heart was about to beat a hole through his rib cage when everything went cold. There was a strange hollow moment and then, there it was, the extraterrestrial. The thing had small hands like claws. It was oddly huddled, hunched to fit into the woods, and still it towered over the treetops. It wore a huge hood and long robe, made from the night from where it came. There was a fetid stink on its hissing breath. Its eyes were red embers like the Sweet Roanoke burning a hole through Tommy's pocket.

They'd never seen a devil like this, not even inside the coal mines, where there was all manner of wicked, scuddling things.

Tommy lit a smoke, passed it around.

In fifty years, official word from the Air Force would be the boys had seen a meteor crash, an aircraft navigation and hazard beacon, and a barn owl. Combined with their fear and their particular latitude, the phantom of the Flatwoods, population 257, briefly appeared.

Reporters would cling to the flying saucer story, and so would film-makers. The Shoney's on the other side of the hills would sell Flatwoods Monster figurines. Video game enthusiasts would spin games and graphic novels from what skeptics dismissed as hick folklore.

But for now, there were just three boys, and an empty sky over the silent woods.

Jesus Christ, said Fred, first to speak, and stepped on the gas.

A Truckload of Apples

after *Pandemic Evolution, Day 4,* Matthew Wolfe (USA) 2020

keepsake / winter king / wild twist / gravenstein / pink pearl / honey crisp / tolman sweet / summerfree / belle boskoop / golden spire / nickajack / northern spy / d'arcy spice / chenango strawberry / cameo / mutsu / gragg / ozark gold / cortland / hokuto / spartan / jazz / papirovka / franc rambour / anna / bailey / admirel / sturmer pippin / otterson / topaz / ginger / delfloga / fuji / gala / macoun / rubin / russet / jonalicious / jubilee / red free / liberty / pink lady / crimson crisp / red delicious / granny smith /

Charlie's Angel

after *Three Dancers,* Pablo Picasso (Spain) 1925

Tara was a dancer with breasts made out of helium. She hunted me down after giving me my first ever lap dance at Chez Charles. Said she loved dancing for the ladies. I couldn't tell you what she was after in me. How her brown skin was almost gold against those beach glass-green satin pajamas. Her perfume is still on my skin. After our awkward first tumble, she ordered a bucket of KFC and we ate it in bed. It felt so American. She threw her phone on the floor when her ex-husband started incessantly buzzing. After I called the taxi, I stood at her window, asked her about the beautiful jade jar with the dragon feet at its base. She looked away for a moment, then came up behind me, kissed me on my neck. Those are my babies, she said, the twins I lost last year. I realized there, somewhere in the bright thrill of her lips on my skin, that the vessel was full of ashes. I never saw her again, and never forgot her, either.

Blindness

after *Therese on a Bench,* Balthus (France) 1939

Matthew Matthews always wore a suit and tie to class. None of the other teachers did. Laura sat at the back, close to the exit, but she watched him carefully when he wasn't looking. There was something effete about him, so tailored and manicured and lean, but even so, something else, potent and powerful. It made her restless.

Canadian history had always been boring, but when Matt was talking about Quebec or the fur traders or the Loyalists or the Red River Rebellion, she sat on the edge of her seat. He also taught psychology, and had written a few books on the subject, so he naturally focused on the characters and their motivations, not on dusty dates and statistics or documents that no one would remember past the exams.

Laura ditched chess and joined the camera club when she found out Matt was the guide. She wasn't particularly interested at first, preferring to paint or write, but he had a way of making the work of photography artists come alive through their biographical stories. He made her see things she would have missed entirely, small details about how the world was knit together. She loved listening to him talk to his camera, cajole it to cooperate and catch something magic. Sometimes she imagined he would want to take pictures of her. She would be colourful one moment, then melancholy. She would be interesting.

Sometimes she would be naked in the pictures. No one had ever seen her naked, and she liked the idea that Mr. Matthews would be the first one.

Laura didn't get into a lot of trouble at school. She was quite skilled at hiding all the things that were wrong, expertly keeping them under the surface. But in the last year of high school, she was caught wandering and acting erratic. She said she didn't know where she was. Someone took her down to the guidance office. Mr. Matthews was on duty. He didn't chastise her or lecture her about getting high. He gave her recordings about Buddhism and some books on Carl Jung, told her that altered consciousness was something to take seriously and not frivolously. She imagined going into that wonder world with him, about how soothing his voice would be during her journey.

Matt told her to come to the office anytime that he was on duty, so she did. She told him things she never told anyone, things about her mother's dissociative episodes, things about how kids at school tormented her because her bestie was gay.

One day she showed him some photos she'd taken that she was especially proud of, a slippery rainbow of minnows at the edge of the lake, the purple asters growing in his backyard.

She felt provocative and confident in that moment, but in the next, it all fell apart. Matt had a strange look on his face and he was holding the pictures as if they were poisoned or dangerous. Everything started to echo and feel far away. His voice was thin and brittle. When were you at my house? he asked her.

She thought of his enchanted gardens, of the old swing covered in vines, of the ancient church bench and all the birdhouses. She liked to sit on that bench and think about him looking out the window, imagine him waving from inside, pulling the curtain to one side and calling her to join him. She imagined him in jeans, barefoot, reading Leonard Cohen poetry and drinking dark wine in a big round glass.

Which time? she asked back. I have lots of pictures of your house.

He must have seen her there, she'd thought, hoped, talking to petals and swallows, coaxing her camera to capture something beautiful just the way he taught her. But from the way he is frozen and furious, she knows now that he hadn't. He didn't see her at all.

Stutter

after text paintings, Derrick Hickman (USA) contemporary

He had a way with words, dropping them and picking them up over and over in stops and starts. You found something there, in the way he would dust them off and start again, in the staccato of syllables, the awkward alliteration, in the consonance of his vivisected vocabulary. He would raise a finger and lower his voice when he needed to summon courage to carry on, then all the words would flow into a warm river of euphony. You wanted him to read to you. You wanted him to tell you your name. How those sharper edges, the first locutions, would give way to a gorgeous tumble of idioms and appellations. You imagined his tongue would taste tart and nervous and fertile, like apples. You wanted him to kiss you, to take the words right out of your mouth.

Karen and Karen

after *The Two Fridas*, Frida Kahlo (Mexico) 1939

for Karen

We were cut from the same cord, a few years apart. Sisters unknown. Rose up in the same wheat fields, same Manitoba snowstorms, and we didn't have a clue. My sister, named the same name. At sixty, helping a dying great aunt look for her daughter, I found the secret that would soon have been buried with our mother. The sister I'd grieved as stillborn all my life. A girl out there. Our mother stayed married to my father for 70 years. It was a rare commitment, a long road of till death do us part, and there was a fork in the road: a mistake and a miracle. *Karen.* From another father. Karen is half me. She does not come into view for many more years. I have found out the secret but have not found *her*. She is real but not real. When I don't hear back, after that first surge of hope, I forget I have put my bottle out to sea. But today, an email. Inside of it, my beating heart. A woman who is also named Karen. We will meet, clandestine like furtive lovers, in hopes of not breaking anything. We will both have lives behind us and sturdy shoes beneath us. We might be sewn together, we might return to life apart, we do not yet know how it is, or how it will go. We only know, we are Karen, two sides of the same coin. Is there something in me that knew I'd been severed from myself, something in her that said so? I do not know. I do not know whether I will click with her or she will click with me. It doesn't matter. Too much time has turned to dust already. There is only blood and rust, there is only the sun setting over the prairies, shorn of brambles and brick by the pioneer women in wagons who came before us.

Tightrope Love

after *The Big Circus,* Marc Chagall (France, b. Russia) 1968

Whipped in white, and wavering, I wade toward the one who wants to tame me. I keep my eyes on his wobbling top hat and think about cake. This too, will fall to pieces, crash below the canopy and into the real world. There will be a few precarious thrills to weather first, before our fall from glory: the tiger cage, the trapeze of desire. And then, he will be a vanishing act and I will be Enormous Norma on the carousel, fattened on corn dogs and cotton candy. The sideshow, juggling clowns.

November Woods

after *Night Woods*, Carl Morris (USA) 1957

Frost is falling across the forest, and the valley is darkening to teal when you finally kiss me. I could hardly wait to find you that way, to press my blue lips against that place of you. It had been years since I'd been kissed at all and maybe it was the same for you but I wouldn't know that until later. We were as startled and stunned as the deer that saw us from the break in the woods. I almost took off after her, the wild thing in me. Yes, before we even started, I was thinking of making a run for it. But I didn't, and you didn't. The doe stood blinking and silent. We were gone so long that even the stars were cold by the time we turned back in.

Kitten Heels

after *Night Bird*, Joan Miro (Spain) 1939

I was telling you how I'd never felt anything about birds for so long. I could not be moved by a sweet chirp or a confident arc of wing. When my father pointed out a swooping hawk, his voice broken by wonder, I would duck back inside a book after a brief glance upwards. I was almost indifferent to the parade of colourful costumes, to feathered masks and tendril plumes, to the tender toes branching three ways over a small berry. My nonchalance shifted on the occasion I found a felled fowl, and a small kitten licking its lips and batting a paw across the bird's tiny fluttering throat. Her heart was a small seed pounding under a tear like a seam down her breast. I was an unwilling witness at the moment that it stopped, and something small but deep changed in me forever. You didn't say much then, you never did, but I could always read what you were thinking. You wanted to share something from the gospel, a snippet of poetry about divine handiwork or the eye on the sparrow, and maybe a word or two about the gulf between glory and pain in nature. I kicked off my little heels and stretched out across your divan with your striped cat and a tumbler of Rioja. You drowned your own small splash in Evian and said you had to get up early. Moved my blue suede shoes to the Wayfair tree in the lobby. Well, if I sometimes wondered what you saw in me at all, it was only the flickering of old fears, small winged demons that sparked through my life like glow fly hummingbirds. I stayed up late watching them glitter across the night at your window. When the sun came up, you were already up waiting for it. Your fingers were covered in paint and your rosary was in a heap on the table. You nodded at me, then, at the coffee machine. It was that space between here and morning, the only place I'd ever been able to find you.

The Garden

after *Number 34,* Jackson Pollock (USA) 1949

The clatter of birds, the scattered blooms. Blue is aching bright over the orchards, with handfuls of cellophane clouds close enough to touch. Here is what I will leave behind: a gaggle of gambolling ducklings, the claret rounds of shy strawberry wilds. The foxgloves and delphiniums are swaying sentries at the edge of the hill. Today there is the sting of fire from behind the apple trees, a truck-bed load of a life smelting to ash. There are mountains more to be hauled to the flames, towers of refuse, dusty brochures and jelly jars, cardboard boxes, newspapers spanning four decades. Already the city dump has turned us away after too many trailers of muck and dross. The thrift stores, too, finally, have kindly pushed back our bounty. Mother is sniffling and ruddy, wringing her hands and cursing us, even as we do all the work. She has not lifted a finger, of course, save to sift through another box of rancid sundries with hopes for salvage. My sister is sorting a heap of rusty wheels and dead electronics for scrap and recycling, and her teenage son is in goggles and gloves, clearing through the fifth freezer. He holds up a bundle of unidentifiable carcass, reads out loud: best before December, 1983. Mother has already hauled off forty-four trailer loads into storage and a half dozen to her new house, too. To his new life, my father took only a small suitcase and his Bible. I have not been here for years, and I will never be here again. We have come apart, we are dismantling, untangling, unravelling. The mounds will follow Mother, spring up wherever she goes. No labour, no fire can erase her, or annihilate her need and her rage. Her poison cannot be razed. Here is what I will take with me: the sweet trill of yellow summer warblers, the small triumph of that temporary demolition.

Darker

after *Abstract Painting (Black),* Ad Reinhart (USA) 1963

The little white house where I unpacked your picnic basket of white wine and Italy, where you laid me back and danced me to the end of love, was more like a grave. The pale tulips in the backyard were a funeral, and the future was murder. But you could never have known that, because I never told you the half of it. I read every single poem in those Leonard Cohen paperbacks you gave to me. And that's why I listened with my all my heart when you said you were in love with me, even if I never really believed you. Of course what you felt was real, no doubt, but it didn't and couldn't change anything. So I let it be, a story spilled on the kitchen floor where I first slipped out of my second-hand silk peignoir, slid out of scuffed slingbacks. I couldn't comfort you in the conflict between you and the woman who hadn't touched you in ten years, but it made me sick to think a sentient soul could leave a loving man like you out in the cold. It was something that struck close to home, how my patient, tender Daddy had been denied everything by Mother, then been tarred and feathered for that longing for connection. He never complained- I only knew it because of her constant reminders that me and my brothers were made by fluke the times that she had bitterly given in. She spat out our names, our lives, with disgust. It made me dark and angry, how sex is so often violence, and not just from the one with the loaded gun.

The Nightingale

after *The Goldfinch,* Carel Fabritius (Netherlands) 1654

for Japey

"Darkling, I listen." John Keats

I dreamed that you would sing something else, that there was still time. If I'd ever thought about it more carefully, I would have guessed you would fall from the edge of the earth. That you would be a Chatterton or Wilde, brilliant and beautiful, eternal puer. With your pure romanticism and all that poetry, it would have been obvious, had it only ever crossed my mind. If not this, you would have been torn apart by lions or poisoned with laudanum or Bella Donna by a jealous suitor. You would suffer the slow dance down, die of consumption, in something purple and velveteen like Wolfgang wore to his last requiem. You would be smashed to terrible pieces in a car crash, or no, a train derailment, just outside of St. Petersburg. Even when I was losing you, I didn't pay any attention. You told me not to- you were planning your new symphony. As if a little old virus was going to stop you. And then you were out like a light, snapped away in a startled blink. I have your voice, still, spooled on an old cassette tape. You were nine, with a falsetto as pure and clear as a castrato, or a goldfinch. It hurts to go back to that time but sometimes I have to, just so I can hear you. From here I can hear what we could not hear then, those tolling bells. We carried on as if we had our whole lives ahead of us.

First Bluegrass Lesson

after *Scales Mound,* John Rogers Cox (USA) 1974

Your guitar is blooming cornflowers. They sprouted without invitation, appeared without warning. You were trying to coax a classical flamenco sound from her strings, something soaked in the sun and a million mosaics. You wore them well, the roomy shirts, those plume-sleeved silky reds. I wouldn't have pictured you in oversize overalls with a blade of grass twisting in your maw, but there we were, in a blue Kentucky field in the middle of a flink of blinking bovine. Well, when I was wee, I'd scrambled down the slopes to the creek bed, parked my imaginary mare on an apple tree. I longed to be Calamity Jane, and I combed that trickling rivulet for wayward bullets or buried bones. But now it was another lifetime, and I was wielding a banjo. You were ignited and jittery, hopped up on marigolds and music. How it zinged through the kernel-strewn mud, fast and furious, into our fingers and through us.

Lepidoptera

after *Taxidermist,* De David Scott Evans (USA) 1881

Pheasant Falls, end of the line. There is only a diner and smoke shop at either end of a triplet of small houses. On the other side, city-potted geraniums and a path to the waterfalls. An arrow points past the narrow choir of pines to the museum.

You have come together from the city to see the birds and the bears, and the butterfly room. You will see mineral specimens, too, a treasure chest of agate and amethyst, geodes and fossils transporting you back in time and deep into the earth. *Sticks and Stones,* a little-known gem of taxonomy.

You come to a dilapidated house, with antlers and boulders strewn through a scraggly garden. There are no signs to confirm you are at the right place, but a cold-faced ibex glares through the window at your approach.

The proprietor is sleazy little man who looks like he should have been an American rattlesnake preacher instead. He is small and sinewy, but his face is pitted and his lips are rubbery. He sprays when he talks. He ushers you in with a sweep of both hands. There are over four thousand specimens of butterflies here, he tells you, fanning at the grid walls, floor to ceiling. This is just a drop in the bucket, he explains. There are more than 180 thousand kinds of lepidoptera. I wanted one of each, he says, but then I started collecting bones, too.

The man is scrubbed to shine, as if his mother still takes fingertips with spittle to his hair, and his halfway undone shirt is pressed and white. All this in contrast to the rooms of reindeer and weasels, undusted for years. *Lloyd.*

You almost understand his passion, his obsession, for fowl and fauna. Yours is for art history, but it is parallel in a way: galleries of still lifes and evolution in painting could be seen as taxidermy of sorts.

Even so, he makes you both uncomfortable with those claw-like little hands of his waving around and also all over you. He thwacks Mike on the back, pushes you both into the next diorama where a grimy moose head greets you with an empty stare. A bear's jaws are propped open in mockery of a threat long ago extinguished.

We don't kill 'em, Mike, Lloyd assures your man, who has been taking close-up photos with his phone. We just collect 'em. He thumps him again. We get a call, you see, one bighorn sheep down, do you want it? And we say yes, we'll take it. His stubby fingers linger for a moment on your upper arm, steal a squeeze.

You see, the big museums, they want whales, dinosaurs, mummies. Lloyd says he'll gladly take a cache of broken crystals or a marsupial that needs work to get back into one piece.

Lloyd is a leading expert on animal cadaver restoration and posthumous surgery. Not so skillful with the living.

To make polite conversation, you say you love rocks, too. You flash your mammoth ring, a chunk of blue and Bedouin pot metal from the Jordanian desert. It might be lapis, or it might be dyed. You know how I tell what kind of rocks? Lloyd asks, taking your hand to better see the specimen you're wearing. Before you or Mike can react, he raises your hand closer, opens his mouth and rakes his tongue, wet and wide and flat across your ring.

You and Mike both freeze, recoil. Lloyd drones on about how you can identify minerals by taste, then something about fixing the wing of the last known passenger pigeon before extinction.

You flee to the ladies' room, washing your prize ring and your hands for a long time. You think about Lloyd, speculate about him growing up unliked by people, retreating into the kingdom before man. You imagine him with a lamp and a needle, putting a small wing back into place, antennae, sorting slides, licking stones, speaking the language of layers of sediments and dead birds.

Bull

after *Bullfight,* Petr Petrovich Konchalovsky (Russia) 1910

after Andres Roca Rey

The matador is a fey little slip of a thing. His smallness is not disguised by the dazzling pale green spacesuit made of light. I'm about to the take the bull by the horns, declare that he needs mothering, but none of the ten thousand ears in the rings would hear me. Kleenex are waving like proverbial ballad lighters in stadiums back home, chins thrust back, braying for blood. My date nudges me, tells me the boy is currently famous for being the worst bullfighter in the world. Just nineteen and already been gored, more times than they can count. I thought I'd read that meeting your maker in a losing match was a badge of honour for a torero, the only way to die. That those never wounded have nothing to show in a game where scars are the currency of manhood. Matteo muffles a guffaw, cups his hand to my cheek with uncharacteristic softness. *Yes, hermosa,* he says, *that is true, but first you have to fell a few bulls.*

Day of the Dead

after *El Señor the de Chalma,* Jose de Mora (Mexico) 1719

Jesus in Mexico, flesh always caught in a fence of thorns, always gaunt-hollow and bleeding. He is tattered in torn purple, crawling to you, beseeching you with upturned claws. You swerve to avoid the lepers and the limbless in the same posture outside of the church, again to duck the old women hawking rosaries and matches. In Taxco, you dodge the throngs in chains and flames, strange rites of un/holy sadomasochism. Maybe we are all penitents, burdened by blackberry brambles, stooped in the searing sun. Maybe we are all bloody angels, festering paws bandaged, ambling to rise up, knock our crutches to the floor. In the cemetery at the south of the city, I come across an altar of bones. There are flies and ivy weaving through the empty sockets of somebody's skull, there are marigolds scattered past the rest of us like coins.

Cages

after *Woman with a Birdcage,* by Jozsef Rippl-Ronai (Hungary) 1892

"I'm holding a lot of power," a friend told me once, and her silver tumble of curls as she cocked her head left a poem forever in my mind. I stirred my tea, waiting patiently for revelation. "I can feel the vibrations, the energy deep in the earth," she said. I hated to kill the mood, but I had to. "I think we all can," I said gently. "This café is right on top of the subway." I pictured her in a velvet gown the colour of dried blood, wading in the sea, the picture of who she wanted to be. Her hands and face were moon pale. She was carrying a birdcage like a lantern.

The Gandy Dark

after *Gandy Bridge, Florida,* vintage postcard, details unknown

Three miles, under moonlight, over the dark bay, long bridge over troubled water. Aside the Sawgrass swamps. The Doors' low groan hypnotic. New Orleans is waiting for you. *Look, I'll drive,* your friend says when you start swerving sideways. You're slipping under, you are fading down to dreams. Yes, you say, stab your fingers into the packet of American Spirit, wave them at the pale pomelo half-plate in the sky, moon lighting your way. You are on your way to meet the Devil you don't believe in, but neither of you know it yet.

A Parable of the Blind Leading the Blind

after *The Parable of the Blind Leading the Blind*, Pieter Bruegel (Netherlands) 1568

"Let them alone: they be blind leaders of the blind. And if the blind lead the blind, both shall fall into the ditch." Matthew 15:14

There is a pale square of eggshell white, an empty space where Bruegel used to be.

It has been removed from the museum, just as many statues, books, speakers, and other artworks have been toppled or torn, ripped from the roots, from city squares or libraries or galleries. The patrons of the historical sites of Naples must learn that their education and edification cannot come at the cost of anyone's hurt feelings.

The image of umbrage is *The Parable of the Blind Leading the Blind,* a five-century old work by the Flemish artist, Pieter Bruegel the Elder. His inspiration was from the gospel of Matthew, when the good Lord warned us about following the dictates of those who didn't know the truth, or weren't even looking for it. The source alone is objectionable to many!

In the painting, assorted men stumble each after one another, grasping and falling on their way. Their eyes are sick or glassy, or not there at all, as if plucked clean by crows, concave sockets, sight hollowed from heads with a cantaloupe baller.

The painting is offensive to people who are blind, or who otherwise identify that way, who might not approve the parallels implied about seeing, the pitfalls of spiritual sightlessness and its insinuated struggles. Peasants and farmers are also furious: this classist assault on the poor and their allies must be erased from memory. Hindus or Jews might be upset by work depicting the New Testament, and the atheists, too, are sick and tired of being force fed life lessons from fairy tale books. Human rights activist groups have asked that all opprobrious religious artwork be removed from the galleries, and curators have their work cut out for them ahead, as forklifts must be brought in to remove countless tons of artefacts from all over the world. All ancient Indian art, all African ritual art, all European Christian art must be tossed onto a bonfire so that aggressions, both micro and intended, can burn in hell. There will surely be some suitably secular moral illustrations from the last two decades that can fill in for the more than ten millennia that human creativity was tainted with faithful delusions.

Some sources report that women are also upset by the piece and have asked to have it destroyed- it looks like the work might have been painted by a *man*.

In an interview with the *Washington Post,* the museum director shared her perspective. "At first, we considered replacing this dangerous work with an appropriate painting from the era or from local contemporary talents. This proved difficult as a staggering number of submissions and backroom stock were equally offensive, if not more so. We thought leaving the blank space was a wonderful statement. And when we overheard a patron expressing how moved she was by the empty wall, we decided to leave it blank with nothing to see. With nothing to look at and nothing to see, it's a safe space for everyone."

Lucky Peace

after *Chinese Take Out,* Heather Ihn Martin (USA) contemporary

The dragon lady is a coiled spring, daring anyone to tempt fate by wandering too close to her windows. In warning, she raps on the dingy glass with crooked fingers. Small jade curios wobble on her side of the barrier, as if they are waving. You are caught up in your SkullCandy TM, tripping over dragonflies and sick beats. Sorry, Mrs Zhao! you call out cheerfully. You still have your last fortune cookie slip from Lucky Peace Diner crumpled in your paratrooper pant pocket: *Best way to get rid of foe is make friend.* Her dowager glower wags wicked and brittle, but you tap your bent fedora, bow a bit, slip her the same sideways smile that makes all the girls melt. And Mrs. Zhao freezes, breaks composure, flashes a brief keyboard streak of grays and whites. Wrinkles her nose a little. For a second, you see the girl she was a million miles ago. Keep smiling! You wave, flitting past on your longboard. Hop off at the lights, stoop to pat a curious beagle. You know what I'm talking about, don't you buddy? you ask. Seriously, man, you ever have that chicken gai ding?

Cuda

after *Barracuda,* Manuel Lopez (USA, b. Cuba) contemporary

His secret is no secret, really. He simply gives the rich white ladies what they want.

It's the best approach, maximizing his scores. The underwater touch on the upper arm, a comment on their hair, or the style of their swimsuit. By now he knows they are ashamed of their pale fat bodies. Some of them wear long t-shirts into the ocean instead of a bathing suit, then tell him it's to keep away the sun. So he uses that inroad, comforts and reassures them. Makes them feel desirable throughout their snorkeling experience. Makes the attraction look like it is his idea, not hers.

Manuel knows European women like to be asked their opinion. The American ones love to show off self-righteous indignation for ecology. For these types he casually brings up the conversation about conservation. He'll mention recent news about the destruction of the reefs, and if he can't recall the details, he'll make them up. He only needs to broach the matter. The women will take over the topic quickly. They will feel important and validated for their trailblazing virtues and astonishing insights.

The next move in his arsenal gives each snorkeller the chance to express herself. As he is doing the safety checks and quick demo on how to use the equipment, he asks each lady what fish she is hoping to see. At least one in each group will say "seahorses," and after a pregnant pause inform him it's her favourite fish because the male is the one who gets knocked up.

This is sort of true, but he doesn't get into it. That will ruin his tips. He will explain instead that it's rare to see them in the reefs. Seahorses don't like commotion, and they tend to prefer vegetation nearer the shore.

Other women will invariably mention angelfish, or the stingray.

Those who have done their homework and really love ocean life will mention the cowfish or lionfish or the fairy basslet. He is more drawn to these women, because they are actually looking at the world around him, and not just at him.

Once he has gone over the obligatory best practice stuff and checked if everyone's gear is in order, they all board the boat for the short ride to the reef. Here is where he'll show something more if he thinks he could stand to sleep with one of them. He will hold her hand a bit longer as he helps her with her balance, sweep his eyes up and down and past her with a practiced nonchalance.

It is what all of them are here for. Not the yellow beaugregory or the trumpetfish, but the dark diver, the bronze and brawny sun-drenched *frijolero*. He will show off his sinewy and strong body, and let his trunks slip just so to reveal the jagged scar under his navel. This long-ago stabbing is a goldmine- it always increases his tips. Even the toughest of tourists are unbelievably sheltered and can't get enough of his scars.

If there is one thing he has learned in all his years of diving and grifting, it is that women love a man with a secret wound.

Sometimes he will bring out the big guns before the girls get into the boat and scare them a little bit by predicting they will see the barracuda.

The ferocious barracuda, only third down in fear royalty from piranhas and Jaws. Predator of the waves. The terrifying *cuda*.

This won't work on everyone. He has learned that the sturdy, flat-footed Germans aren't afraid of anything. Not cartel bosses, not jihadis, not gonorrhea. Unlike the Aussies and the English, they're never ashamed of their ugly calves or their wrinkles. They are as pragmatic as doctors. They are simply not frightened by the four-foot, wieldy-toothed carnivore fish.

Same thing with the Texas broads. One brassy blonde actually pulled a mini revolver out of her deep-sea nylon carry all pouch. Will this work if I see the cuda? she asked, taking all of his power out of the moment.

But it works wonders on the tamer targets. Throw a little fear into the water, and those bikinis are practically fighting to free their buoys.

The barracuda is not as terrible as he seems. He preys on reef life, so of course he is found where the food is. He seldom comes for tourists and even less for locals, and he has only swallowed a few fingers in his day.

But when Manuel uses the cuda story, chances are one or more of his charges will make her move. Tuck an American twenty into his hand, invite him to the hotel bar.

Finished with today's tours, he waits now for the French woman and her friend to finish showering.

This won't be as bad as usual. French women are attractive, even the older ones. They have a reputation here of being stingy with their wallets, but in Manuel's experience, they are generous with the sugar when satisfied. And doing two at once means a little novelty, so he can more easily feign a thrill.

He wishes he was home, sure, showing his young son how to season tamales, or drawing cartoon cudas with his little girls.

He'd rather not go through with it at all. But for tonight, for this time, at least he'll be able to get it up.

Found Objects

after *Pandemic Evolution Day 38,* Matthew Wolfe (USA) 2020

We were on the outskirts of Libson. We walked and walked and walked, when we were still allowed to walk outside. The day was long and gray and the mist rolled down the hills from the castles to the coast, down from Sintra onto the silver strip of shore. A few grills were set up in the sand, and women were selling sardines. We watched the surfers riding steely waves. You gathered glass and barnacles, collecting them in a blue jar. And I tossed someone's broken sunglasses back into the sea. The sun was bobbing red behind the day, playing shy on the other side of the clouds. I loved watching you raise your face to the sky, reaching to touch it. I couldn't believe that you found me, and that I was here beside you. Maybe we would never go back, that's what you were thinking or hoping. The world was about to fall apart, close in on itself, but there was no way we could know. We did not duck to dodge the dendrites of disease; there were no masks, no fears of contamination, no signs warning us to keep our distance from everyone else. All that was true was the sea and the sky, a paper bag of pastéis de nata, and pale frost slivers of flotsam beach glass, like moonstone gifts spangled across the shore.

Havoc

after Franz Kline

Pigment after impression, energy, or flame. A careening scream in paint. The gestural, the spare, wrought epic by sheer magnitude. All the force of love and war in black and white.

Barn

after *Brandon Barn,* Warren Kimble (USA) contemporary

I'm surrounded by apples. The buckets are heavy laden, spotting the front and sides of the barn with mounds of red rounds. David's saws settle in behind the bounty. He points to tomato vines weaving a fence on a heap of boards, to other cauldrons blooming his brother's favoured seeds. The air is full of saw dust and skunk and Jonamac must and the sugar of warm raspberries. David shows me the jigsaw and what he is making. He hacked down the dying walnut tree himself, clawed it from the dirt with his hands and his tools, and here it is, transformed into chess: a raw rook, a crooked king, near perfect pawns. David built the barn we are in, figured out how to fit the pieces together and raise them with his own two ruddy hands and instructions from his Dad and his granddad. He is 20. He has a slow grin and a sharp twinkle behind his glasses. When he was two, he padded over to me with an orange extension cord wound expertly around one arm, pressed the other end to my neck and made animated noises. Started digging holes and mixing cement that same summer, in his floppy yellow boots. He never cried, not until two decades had fallen away and he and I were standing together at the foot of a hospice bed, saying goodbye to my father. Dad, I said, the barn. If you could only see this kid's barn! He never would. He never walked again. We buried him. But in the midsummer sunset, the rooster weathervane raised to that roof brands the night in his blood.

Ruby Slippers

after *The Hatred*, Pietro Pajetta (Italy) 1896

"I will say that in 26 years of law enforcement it's the worst thing I have ever seen." Police Sgt. Aaron Pomeroy

for Ruby Wallick

Nine decades under her belt, but there was still room to spare. Ruby was spry, sharp, and sure of three more years. Even with porcelain bones, light as air. She'd seen it all before, but not this. Who could guess their last supper would be tonight, with Ruby the main course? Her daughter dropped by to drop off fresh rhubarb and some green beans, hoped her mother had the back burner simmering with bacon and spuds. How a crumble of biscuit sopped on steaming top would melt her troubles away. You were never too old to need your Mama, were you? she thought as she climbed the old steps. The cities were in flames around her, and the deadly virus of 2020 was felling her neighbours like branches snapping away. She heard the sounds of struggle, a low and guttural rumble, as if a wild animal had gotten inside. Her call was answered with a strange silence. There was a scuttling noise on the floorboards above. She picked up pace, came face to face with a nightmare: a vampire straddled over Ruby, tearing handfuls of meat from her carcass with both hands. His mouth was stuffed full of fat. He licked his chops, crooked a greased finger her way. Ruby was long gone, emptied into dark pools seeping through the floorboards, eyes fixed on the ceiling. Her slippers were obscenely asunder, red and fuzzy and floating in blood. The sirens were already singing on the outskirts, circling the unrest, scooping up the casualties and injuries. She must have called someone, because they came closer. It took four cops to pry Ruby's grandson from her corpse and a taser for him to release her entrails from his teeth. How do you bury a nonagenarian who has been eaten alive? How do you tell the others that the wolf in the attic was your own?

Cliff Hanger

after *The Chains That Free Us,* Cindy L. Sheppard (USA) 2017

The six of swords, the five of orbs. Things are looking grim. You pull another card, half hoping for a ten of anything or maybe one of the more nurturing goddesses, but it is the hanged man. Look, you have a story to tell and it will keep appearing until you tell it. Stories are like that; they stand in the corner like haunts, long and patient and lonely. Think of the chains you noticed threading along the red cliff walls. Didn't you say then, this feels like a sign?

Death in Tepito

after *Aztec Deities Mictecacihuatl and Mictlantecuhtli, Codex Borgia* (Mexico) 1500s

And just like that, you are there again, pushing your way through the yellow tents of Tepito's market. You cannot stay away from Mexico. It is like skydiving, or popping amphetamines. It is life at the crescendo. These stalls of towering flowers, these heaps of chintzy, absurd toys are a labyrinth connecting the Centro Historico with the no-go barrio. Here, heads roll, if they're lucky.

At the north and east corner of the squalor of caged dogs and baby birds, past baskets of chipotle crickets and nopales, past skyscraper shoeboxes of wrestling masks and diablito figurines, you slip into the streets.

You shake your head curtly whenever a twin set of stony eyes latch onto yours. You aren't looking for blow or a guerrilla machine gun for a steal. You have no list of enemies you want dead.

But you ARE looking for death, after all, and haven't you always been? Tonight, you are one of her pilgrims.

You follow the others past the shady men whose faces are covered like old western train bandits. Toss paper money into an upturned cup for an ancient mestiza missing both legs. She hands you a bouquet of orange and violet chrysanthemums. Armed with sacred offerings, you are now part of the procession. A thousand candles flicker as the river of humans moves toward Her shrine.

You approach the church of Santa Muerta, a humble hole now showered in purple and gilt fire. You weren't expecting to see glory in the grim one's gaunt visage, but you were hoping for *something*. A glimpse, at least, of what might come after. But the colours in her aura are festoons of the living. There is nothing there after all, only sockets emptied of sight, and a grinning rope of clattering dentin keys.

The Hell Cat

after *Cat Devouring a Bird,* Pablo Picasso (Spain) 1939

The occasion that Spencer came and left, I almost broke my teeth biting down on Jolly Ranchers. It was the time of quarantine: I badly wanted a creature to love again, and assumed it would be enough. But he was a wild thing. He'd been left to his own devices in the concrete jungle I called home, and now he couldn't comprehend that fish and fuzzy blankets were his for the taking. The stress of his suffering drove me to drink, but midway down a glass of Shiraz I was half soused and nauseous and wanted my own mind. My nerves were frazzled and I was desperate for oxygen. If he could have just taken a sip of water or a morsel of chicken in those tense 24 first hours, I could have turned in with a racy mystery and an Ativan and let sleeping dogs lie. But my senses were jarred into overdrive, parallel to his terror, and I was choking on the anxiety and racing with adrenaline. The creature was climbing the walls, hair on end, mouth jagged and agape, like something out of Transylvania. I popped a watermelon lozenge first, then a blue raspberry, crushing them between my molars with a vengeance. An old and badly patched cavern cracked a little more. Just a fracture somewhere between gold and bone and sugar. In the night, the ache awakened me and I spat shards of blue jelly and a few enamel tendrils into the sink. There was a hole in the window screen and a handful of black and white fur stuck to the gash in the wires. Spencer was gone as quickly as he came, as if he'd never had a chance. I questioned everything in that moment, if love could cure anything, if safety was always a mirage, if grief over nature's brutality was really empathy or just a mass delusion. I wanted to be as tough as my mother, who once conquered the vicious snapping turtle attacking her geese. She wrung his neck with her bare hands and made him into soup without flinching. I wanted to be tough like my father, whose reasoned softness was just the frosting on steely resoluteness. I wanted to look at life and death with the same sturdy peasant blood as they did, but all I had was anguish and poetry. I was all hope and impulse and wound. The ragged tear in my mouth started throbbing and I fumbled for Aspirin, for anything harder. But the kibble and the tuna were still untouched; and the kennel carrier was empty. Spencer was gone, and now in more danger, like everything else I'd ever tried to save.

Pho

after *Nighthawks*, Edward Hopper (USA) 1942

Easter is cancelled. We are separated by the novel coronavirus. We will not break bread this year, we will not pray together around the table with our niece and nephews and our sister. It is a hole in my heart. Our last supper was a bowl of tripe, smothered in hoisin and sriracha. We were at Pho Del Bau, where years ago an irate old woman caught us smoking pot behind someone's van in the parking lot. She threatened to call 911. The best we could do was slink past her, turn to shadows on the side street running behind the fence, zig zagging lanes until we lost her. Then, reclaiming the utilitarian warmth of the camp-style tables, we landed, giddy from the chase and frost and smoke. The tendon soup was salty sustenance, and the green tea brought us down to the table we had come for. Maybe it was the little burst of adrenaline in the adventure that cemented it for us, or maybe it was the steaming heaps of cheap noodles, but the plain pho hall on that corner became our place. Whenever I came back, we would go, talk about where we'd gone and what we'd done and what we hadn't done, slip away for a sip of our own. I couldn't tell if the end of the world was nigh, but it was coming closer than ever before. This time, I told you I was certain that a quarantine was coming, and I wouldn't be back home for awhile. I said, *if this is it, know this cumin cup of broth with you is the most important thing there is.* That is how it has been for me since you were born. You always had a shell-shocked expression, even when you were two and I was fifteen. It is this face I see now, the same face I saw at our father's deathbed, when you looked straight at me and said, *now for sure, if it weren't for you, I really would be totally alone.* And you turned back to him, pulled the sheet over his cold teeth. His hand still in yours. I saw in that terrible silence how the knuckles were knobby, and fingers slim, like yours, like mine.

Running Hot and Cold: Variations

after *Interior,* Vilhelm Hammershoi (Denmark) 1899

1. You awake from idyllic dreams into the fire. If you once curled up, cocooned, under a festival of crochet squares, festooned by plush sentinels, just shy of the licking edges of her flames, now by middle age, you can sleep with the lights off.

2. But just like that, the world is coming apart at the seams. The streets are crawling with infectious enemies crowned in dizzy dendrites looking for another host to fell. But you won't fall, will you? You who have overcome everything, even death, even the descent into the Hades of human madness. You walked through hell, held out the life float in vain to many melting into stalactites, witnessed the nightmare of your men eroding in the smoke of methamphetamine. All that panic, all that scramble, claws grasping sanity before the ultimate demise. You kept his meth pipe, shrouded in a white cloth at the back of a drawer of dust and other memories. If anyone who saw the thing would ask why you kept this instrument of darkness, you would have said this: to be able to look evil in the face, to remember, without flinching.

3. *Vilhelm Hammershoi.* The artist from Denmark. The stovepipe in the corner has long cooled, but the woman in the long black dress is unmoved. She is always reading some letter, or drying her hands on her apron, or tilting her head in

a way suggestive of some soft sorrow. Her naked nape makes you feel like you are eavesdropping.

4. She is all there is in all of her husband's paintings. All, that is, besides the angled planes of floorboards, or doorways, or the lines and quarters of windows and empty picture frames. She is the chair and the book and the canvas that sometimes appear; she is the curved carved bone of the piano leg, and the teacup and the book and the urn.

5. She is the wooden lady of his ship, that solitary vessel in the gray expanse of ocean. Once, before he loved her, there was something else, another marker that defined him. It was about finding a man in the orchard, crooked at the neck, almost broken, dangling from the branches. His hand was, in that strange sleep, upturned, open, not in petition, exactly, but still, asking for something.

6. Perhaps it is the key to why all of his work feels like a ghost story.

7. The young man who would be an artist stood sentry in those spring blooms, not turning until the world turned, and morning was broken. He never went back, but even so, he never left those silent woods.

8. In the heat of the moment, entropy, collapse. An avalanche of pyramids crashing down. You have sucked on soap as if it was a teat, tried to wash something putrid and bitter from your palate. If sticks and stones can hurt you, words lacerate and burn. As the world burns, friends should be a lifeline,

not turn on each other. In all that private fury, what you wouldn't give for mere cold floors, unkindness.

9. If Van Gogh was drowning in chartreuse and violets, and Picasso was a hotheaded bison of a man, the great Dane was cool and serene. His world was barren of bawdy words or festering infections. He bleached everything to bland, swept every room free of intimation. His simplicity put monks to shame. Any spice, he froze to white. His palate was black and white and grey. His rooms were empty of everything but memory.

10. A century later, the world falls silent again. All the doors shutter, factories fall, planes stay grounded, churches are closed until further notice. Only the hospitals have crowds.

11. You slept like a baby the Monday after the city declared a state of emergency. The rest of the world already had: Covid-19, 2020. You had cached four weeks of tuna and pickles, four months of cat food and Tampax, and cashed in four hours of tears already spent. And bullets. You never thought about your Daddy's rifle in the safe you'd never once cracked open, but now you did think about it. Wondered if things might escalate out there into the kind of world where you'd be grateful just to have it.

Promiscuity

after Tom of Finland

If Amir was home, I wore pajamas in case I had to pee at two in the morning. More than once, more than a hundred times, I encountered a stranger in the night, in my own halls, some guy awkwardly zipping in a hurry or fumbling with his boxers, as I approached my own bathroom in search of relief. My roommate was alone for as long as I knew him, and often talked about love, but he had a fist tattooed on his forearm and an ink whip winding around the other, and he always went out on the prowl after studying. Sometimes his lovers' leather boots were jumbled outside his room, while he and whoever banged away against his thin door like two cats at a Mixed Martial Arts competition. Sometimes when I found him stirring the broad beans for *foule* in the morning, Amir had burns from the poppers on his face or hands. He wasn't daunted by the spook of HIV, and when it happened, it didn't slow his hunger or change his sensibility one bit. He would just don chaps and chains and slink into the streets below, dragging home whatever scraps would find him. I don't know if he found or used the condoms I left on the map of Egypt in his room. If I cared, what could I say? I had my own compulsions to contend with.

One night, stealing in, saturated in tequila with my own lost causes, I found the house dark but for flickering candles and the mournful timbre of Nina Simone's "In the Dark." I followed her low growl into the living room and saw Amir, slumped, catatonic, in a soiled undershirt and little else, his lenses sparking back a dozen tealight flames. When I leaned in with a warm hand and a murmur, he did not retreat. When I asked if he was okay, he took off his specs, polished them on the ribbed cotton of his wife beater, and bore into me with an agony I never did let go of. His other side, the scholar who ate books with the same hunger that he devoured men, the broken poet who would trail his finger along sacred lines of ancient Arabic script and weep at their beauty, crumbled to tears. "I've just never been able to reconcile my promiscuity with my faith," he said. It was the only time he ever spoke about that particular intersection. For one split second, there was a silence in the world, then Nina's voice caught, slipped, changed gears. Amir lit a cigarette, drew deep, exhaled. The kettle started keening in the kitchen behind us, and the moment was gone.

Online Quarantine Curiosity Cabinet, Amazon Edition

after *Pandemic Evolution Day 21,* Matthew Wolfe (USA) 2020

2020 Order History, Amazon:

Still Life with Oysters and Lemon: On Objects and Intimacy, by Mark Doty / Pro Pets Probiotics for Dogs and Cats / Ten Holes Twenty Tones Blue Harmonica Key of C For Beginners, Kids, and Musicians / Cannibalism, Headhunting and Human Sacrifice in North America: A History Forgotten, by George Franklin / Travel Qwirkle / Art Chronicles, by Frank O'Hara / Black Micron Gel Fine Liner Pen Set / The Oxford Book of Latin American Short Stories, Edited by Roberto Gonzalez Echevarria / Food Grade Diatomaceous Earth 2.2 Pounds / Deluxe Extra Volume Big Space Weekly Pill Organizer Rainbow Variety / Prisms Clear and Blue Glass Pleasure Enhancer with Nubs and Swirls / The Penguin Book of the Prose Poem, From Baudelaire to Anne Carson, Edited by Jeremy Noel-Tod / Screw Eyes Zinc Plated Metal Eye Shaped Screw, 191 Count / Inktopia Printer Cartridges with New Updated Chip / How to Fly (In Ten Thousand Easy Lessons: Poetry, by Barbara Kingsolver / Perfect Desiccated Liver Grass Fed Undefatted Argentina Beef / Black and Decker Two Slice Toaster Red Blowout Clearance / Arte Popular: The Rex May Collection of Mexican Folk Art, From the Mexican Museum / Serrapeptase Enzymes / After Hours, by Darrell Epp / Yesterday's News Compressed Cat Litter 35 Pound Bag, Recurring / Atlas Obscura, Second Edition: An Explorer's

Guide to the World's Hidden Wonders, by Joshua Foer et al / The Dead Kid Poems, by Alexis Rhone Fancher / Stash Peach Black Tea Bags 100 Count / Sharp Objects, by Gillian Flynn / Simple Table Lamp Bedside Desk Baby Book Case or Night Stand / Twelve Pack 3x3 Inches Painting Craft Stretch White Blank Canvas Panels Mini Artist Small Acrylic Oil Famous Artist / My Favorite Things: 75 Works of Art From Around the World, by Sister Wendy Beckett / Cuff Daddy Maine Lobster Cuff Links, Silver Plated

Night Swimming

after *Two Ladders,* Gertrude Abercrombie (USA) 1947

A bottle to the sea, a ladder to the sky. Those slim rungs won't hold you, that sliver of moon will slice in two the hand it hooks. You can swim with the gulls and hide from the owls, you can tell all of your stories to the pale cat who follows. But you can't see yourself in the mirror in the dark or breathe under water. Your scroll won't be found until you have turned into seaweed and shells. You will return as a drowned horse or a woman who points at windows and doors. You will forget everything but the quickening branches, jittery, frail, shaking their fists at the moon.

Pulp Fiction

after vintage *True Detective* cover art

I just wanted to be with him, the detective. That's why I spent night after night curled up inside, happy to give up my world for a few hours and live in his. Those steely eyes, that resigned cut of mouth, all business, yet with something of the walking wounded in him. All women have yearned for his mind and his heart and those biceps. Television magic. We can commune with the archetypes. We want the detective so bad that we settle for fiction because it's true. Whoever he is, brooding yet goofy, loves cats, loves jazz, good wines, makes killer tacos. Bosch, D'Onofrio, Patrick Jane. Figures out puzzles, looks evil in the eye without flinching. Has a spare Glock in his waistband, knows how to use it.

Mrs. Jones

after *Lunch at the Restaurant Fournaise,* Pierre Auguste Renoir (France) 1879

Mrs. Jones wrests apart her fortune cookie with a click of a callous, pries loose the truth with fake fingernails and admirable dexterity. A crackle of crumbs tumbles down her lapel, into the leftover rice. Her date waits word, awaits his fate, with the mildly bored expression of an enamoured paramour used to his object of amusement. What now, Mrs. Jones? he asks, reaching for the paper that will dictate what happens next. Mrs. Jones purses her soy-smeared lips, gives him a coy, sidelong glance, hands him the verdict. *Better luck next time*, it is written.

Triskaidekaphobia

after *Thirteen Rectangles,* Wassily Kandinsky (Russia) 1930

1. Twelve gods walk into a bar. They clink tumblers of mead, pass platters of herring and oatmeal. No one thought to invite Loki, who shows up anyways, sows chaos that ends with an arrow shooting and poison mistletoe. Norse story. Dinner party from hell.

2. Nancy Drew is kidnapped again, after searching for the rare and valuable *Thirteenth Pearl* in Tokyo. It is her last adventure, at least, until the next franchise in her name.

3. Grade ten poetry class: thirteen ways of looking at "Thirteen Ways of Looking at a Blackbird."

4. A bigger mouthful: *paraskevidekatriaphobia.* Fear of Friday the 13th. A syncretic superstition- Good Friday turning bad, and merging with 13. A 20th century phenomenon, and not universal: Tuesday the 13th is worse, in Spanish.

5. Thirteen is good luck, too. A star or stellate number in mathematics.

6. Bar Mitzvah, thirteen, marking the age of maturity and a full member of the Jewish faith, where God has Thirteen Attributes of Mercy.

7. A talisman of fortune and chance in France, popular on old postcards.

8. *Fare tradici-* "make thirteen" in Italian. Means "to hit the jackpot."

9. The lunar calendar has thirteen months in a year. The menstrual calendar, also.

10. The Mayan calendar used thirteen-day measurements for time.

11. The thirteenth card of the Tarot's Major Arcana is a skeleton with a sickle: the grim reaper, death.

12. There are thirteen constellations of stars in astronomy, and only twelve zodiac signs in astrology.

13. An observant child in an elevator points out that the buttons are missing a floor. His Dad explains that real estate sometimes omits thirteen and goes to fourteen because some people think the number thirteen is bad luck. The kid processes all that, blinks, then blurts, "Call it what you want, it's still going to be floor thirteen." True story.

Jalapeños

after vintage chilli pepper posters

You were too hot to handle, I said, trying to make light with corny clichés. But you could not be consoled. It was hard to accept that anyone had the power to upset you so profoundly, somebody other than me.

You had this thing for chili peppers; once, I got you these festive little patio lights shaped like jalapeños. You plugged them in and fired up the BBQ. You tossed some ribs and some red-hots on the grill. We were panting after a few charred masterpieces. You poured Chardonnay over ice and we watched the night rise and the cars go by.

What does it say about me to admit that the times we walked the train tracks at dawn were the best days of my life? You once got me drunk enough to kiss you, behind the ATM machine at the Winchester Arms. We both had boyfriends. In daylight, we trekked every inch of rail that ran through this county, throwing pebbles at trains from bridges and the overpass behind your cousin's farm. You always played the Will You Still Love Me If game when we were watching trains. If I was fat, if I had a lisp, if I was a ruthless CEO… As if. I couldn't live without loving you. On our roams, you always wore white and red striped socks and a Polaroid camera around your neck. I would have done anything to be with you forever.

Sometimes, I don't know what I'm thinking, you say, jostling me back to the present. You get too intense sometimes, as if the world ignites to flames.

Well, you don't scare *me*, I blurt.

You nod. Well, thanks, you say. Even so, you want to get a grip, find a way to keep your cool, stop hurting people. You say you are too volatile, spinning off the chart with the slightest provocation.

I imagine putting a cold cloth on your forehead, dipping your ravaged nails into antiseptic and bandaging them carefully.

I remember once when you'd come home after taking off for the ocean. You showed me scars on your wrists, and I thought they were beautiful like feathers.

Today your shirt is black and neon pink and says *hot stuff,* emblazoned in stencil type.

I tell you to down a handful of Valium and some wine, our reliable vices. You'll feel better in the morning, I say. But you say you're tired of all that. You are tired of going off the deep end. You think something is wrong, that you need help, and you think it could be empowering to take some responsibility.

I want to tell you that all this damage, this fever pitch of you, is what I crave. The rush of you. I can't imagine you otherwise.

It never occurred to me that you did not love these things as I did, and in one strange moment that I realize I do not want you to find your way out.

A terrible worry ignites deep inside me. I wonder if I want you to be sick because I am.

That's how I loved you, I want to scream. But you know nothing of the things that I've kept hidden.

Tiny Dancer

after *Two Ballet Dancers,* Edgar Degas (France) 1879

The drum and bass is relentless, pounding a hole in my head. I slip outside of the swarm to come and find you. You are rinsing your tiny feet in my sink, jostling them to and fro in dish soap bubbles. *I feel like a ballerina,* you say, hiking up your cuffs and letting the tap flow over. All is quiet for a moment. The motion is outside of us. I marvel at how compact you are, how you can fold yourself into the second sink like a Buddha. Even your lamps have these same clean lines. I am always everywhere, fumbling, falling, stumbling, and that's how I am now, worrying anxious fingers through my pockets to find a vial or baggie, something to sustain us. You have turned our whole home into a gallery for my art works, and now the city streets are streaming inside and looking at us. The edges of the world have turned up, waiting for us to mix them a martini. It is too early for us to know where exactly we are going or how we have arrived at this point. I hope one day to go with you to all those yellow churches in Peru, but have no way yet of knowing it will come to pass. I don't know either that most of our dreams will fall apart, or that 20 years from today we will reconvene on Yonge Street for thin crust pizza, sober. I take your small back, guide you to ground, pass you a straw. We slip back into the frenzy and the noise. We don't yet have a clue what we have wrought so far, what we will survive.

Checkers

after *May Picture,* Paul Klee (Switzerland) 1925

Klee plays checkers, blue, white, blue, white, blue. Each square staccato, tap step soliloquy, spin swirl, cymbal brush. You are a dizzy witness, toes tipped in fire. You can't keep. You can't stay. You have things on that list, you have people to see. The sky is waiting. Don't keep her waiting.

Outlaw Shit

after *A Dash for the Timber,* Frederic Remington (USA) 1889

1. Steve's mother was a killer redhead. She had tresses so long and red I was sure she was Juice Newton. She was tall and lean in denim, with a slow and rusty voice. I wanted her armour armload of bangles.

2. They didn't live far from our house, so I sometimes rode my bike over, with the pretense of doing homework. Janine was in the same math class and sometimes we even opened our textbooks. Mostly, I just wanted to moon over her older brother. Wished I could touch his curls. I loved watching Alice pick up the golden decanter when night started to fall over the scraggly pear trees just outside the window. I loved the smell of the gin, and the cigarette haze.

3. She would drink and listen to Waylon Jennings records. *Someone called us outlaws in some old magazine...*It felt like a refuge from how my own mother was yelling all the time, belittling and blaming my patient, quiet father for everything, taunting him with her affairs. Someone else's garbage always seems more romantic when you are only eleven.

4. One afternoon, I saw a man's work boots outside of her door. Asked Janine if they belonged to her father. "I wouldn't know," she said, chewing on the end of her pen. "I've never met him."

5. I was too young to ride on the back of Steve's dirt bike but I went anyways, felt my pulse quicken at the noisy rev of motor and the lightning jolt between his Iron Maiden T-shirt and my small hands. Thought about Alice's blood in his veins, and it made me dizzy.

6. In the shed, that shallow barn now fallen to small finches and blackberry vines, Steve finally kissed me.

7. It was a brotherly brush of his new stubble against my cheek. It sent me flying. His lips barely touched me, a mile from my mouth. No matter. I carried that moment like a trophy for years to come.

8. That sprawl of freckles under his eyes.

9. There was no follow up kiss. No real kiss. Not for my lack of trying. Steve said he liked me, but I was too young. Then one day, he was taken off to juvenile detention. Alice didn't seem perturbed or surprised. She just laughed in that throaty noise of hers, handed me her overflowing ashtray. Be a doll, she said, wiggling her pointy nails at the trashcan.

10. Janine cried, said there were B&E charges and a stolen car. Said now there was no one to make dinner, and she would have to learn to make sandwiches and use the oven.

11. For a year or so, I sent letters to Steve. He wrote out his affection for me and the mundane events of his days in stubby pencil scrawl. I would lurk at the end of the gravel lane, camped out in the milkweed ditch, waiting for them.

12. When my breasts rose up overnight, I wept for want of showing them off to him. Imagined pressing them into his back on that bike, my hand finding the damp space between my thighs while I dreamed of it.

13. I didn't see Steve again until I was seventeen. We had lost touch but after some old country records dusted off my memories, I tried to find him. By then, he was in the real prison. I was old enough, my folks decided, to visit him. I signed in on the list, sat in the strange glaring lights of the institution with the other jail groupies, until they called my name and led me through a maze of locked doors and metal turnstiles. The whole time, my father waited prayerfully in the parking lot for me to find my way back to him.

14. I went faithfully to see Steve, counting the days each week, counting the hours. I began to live for those thirty-minute sessions, separated by plexiglass. I wasn't fazed when I found out Steve was serving time for stabbing a guy with an ice pick. I was safer with the outlaws than I was around my own mother. Their kind of cruelty was visceral and predictable. They might even defend you. You knew where you stood.

15. One day, just like that, Steve told me he would stop writing and no longer accept my visitation requests. I died inside. When I asked if it was someone else, he shook his head. Told me he lived for my letters, kept my smile beside him when he slept. I was a beautiful young woman, he said, and it was wrong for me to waste my life waiting for him.

He knew that it would hurt me, but also knew that one day I'd look back and see that he was right.

16. Years later when I asked my father why he'd taken me there, he said he knew I would have gone anyways, without him. Daddy was at soul a preacher man, but he'd always told me there was more decency among cons than church men. He wasn't surprised that Steve decided not to drag me under, the way he hadn't taken advantage of me when I was just a kid, when he had the chance. The way he looked after his little sister.

17. I might still have them, somewhere, his letters.

Hebe

after *Mrs. Wells as Hebe,* Thomas James Northcote (England) 1805

Mrs. Wells watches from the helm of the museum's hallowed halls, shimmies off her shawl, yields her slippy sleeve to the vulture's beak. I'm with the bird- I too would stroke the soft hollows of Mrs. Wells's elbow and decolletage. She is powdered in perfume, in lavender and amber. She is what we all long for, this Mrs. Wells. Wide-eyed wonder and pale pink lips curled in a half-smile, soft thighs apart a little. If we just touch her, we could find forever.

The Keychain Monkeys

after *Afternoon at the Zoo*, James Grant (USA) 1950

The zookeeper always watched for the girl in the yellow dress. She walked up to the boulevard and past the bougainvillea every school day around three, on the other side of the fence. He would fiddle with the faucets at the vantage point of sighting, rinsing slop buckets or filling bottles, until he saw her. She was always alone, like him, not part of the gaggles of gangly limbed girls as noisy and mean as the geese they marched past on the other side of the zoo. He was friendly with those kids anyways, lifting his hat or tossing off an awkward wave. Some of them mocked him for his limp or stutter, but mostly they didn't notice him at all. They were looking for the baby tigers or the meerkats on their way home. The girl in the yellow dress always stopped where she did in hopes of a glimpse of the pygmy marmosets, still and intent for a long time on the other side of their enclosure. Their preferred quarters was a box nestled in the backdrop of blooms, but if you stood in the slight parting of greenery adjacent you could find them. She always called out to him if she saw him, pestered him with questions about their names or their natural habitat. She listened patiently when he stumbled over the answers, waiting for him to find the words. The girl called the creatures the keychain monkeys because they were so small, like ornaments. He loved her pale little hands on the fence between them, her skinny fingers, and the jumble of too many teeth in her small rosebud mouth. He loved the mop of curls she sometimes pinned back with flowers. Once one of the gardeners overheard their chatter and gave him a pitiful, disgusted look. He was mortified, and it took all of his courage to speak up and correct him. You've got it all wrong, he said. She's the spitting image of her mother.

Night Sax in Mexico City

after *Night Sax in Mexico City,* Lorette C. Luzajic (Canada) 2017

I just had one glass of vino but was feeling it, the way I was feeling the blues that came on when I flicked open a playlist. It was the humidity, likely; it was choking me all afternoon. The Pino Grigio was briefly brisk, then melting to puddles between my flushed fingers. I'd been thinking too much since morning, about the rising Covid numbers and the looming rent, and whether to go with blue and orange again in a new painting. And Mexico. I was longing for it like a lover. There was a night roof overlooking the cathedral. They were playing Mexican trance. You could sip mezcal and survey the zocalo, the spread of the city in the heady undertow of the darkness. But for now, I was just here, surrounded by the rest of what I loved, orange cats and white wine and yellow roses from my lover. What would the world be like, after 2020? America was burning up and falling down, and the parks were turning into mass graves. I wanted to blink and be there, in Tlaxcala, soaked in hibiscus water in an oversize tumbler, kneeling before a broken saint. The church would be raucous with gold and lepers. I wanted to fly over our empty cities and into the tempestuous, flower-festooned arms of that place. I wanted to get back there, but there was no going back.

The Paper Dark

after *A Northern Night,* Franz Johnston (Canada) 1917

Winter had already taken hold. The sharp edge of the frost was hard and beautiful, and there was a glass moon rising in the sapphire dark. You brought with you a smattering of pinprick stars and snowy treads from the long and lonely hike to find me. The house smelled faintly of oranges when you entered. You could hear the world arguing downstairs with Tucker Carlson and my father. I had already helped my mother clean up from supper, but there were small noises of busy coming from the kitchen as she prepared the citrus glaze for the coffee cake, and our night-time tea. You caught me finishing my face with a sweep of rose gold in the mirror at the end of the hall, and when our eyes got caught just for a second I knew everything you wanted to speak in words and maybe even would. Well, I promised you that I would always try to act like an adult but I was actually going to kill you right then. I felt wanted and loved and it was shaky ground for me. There you were, having huffed enough bravura to finally say something. But I'd been comfortable in hiding and now I wanted to fold back into myself, to move like a ghost through the walls and back into the endless drifting snow. In the falling sun before you arrived, I'd stepped out of the empty corridor and slipped down into that dark wide space behind the earth. It felt thin and fragile as paper. I watched two men pass by with a sled on the ice, and no one else around for miles. Courage comes in different ways- mine was how I'd finally knit a sort of fence or maybe a moat, a buffer zone, around a woman who had never had any skin. I kept myself apart, wisely steering clear of disaster. Now such defences seemed philistine and uninteresting. You weren't buying it: you were not here to save me or to drown me. You were jumping off your own cliff, head first, eyes wide open, your hands clasped awkwardly mid-air, in ridiculous trust or petition for safe landing.

Tower of Horses

after *Tower of Blue Horses*, Franz Marc (France, b. Germany) 1913

Familiar setting, the city night, the dim bar. The lonely hum of café voices. There were writers, and drummers, and drifters, and a retired postal service worker. He hadn't left his seat since noon, or was it yesterday? Against the back wall, an old pinball machine on its last legs, and a poster of Calamity Jane. She balanced a gallon of bourbon casually on one palm. There was a lamp of Lucite horses glowing indigo, a kind of Coney Island carousel, and that is where I knew I would find you, if I ever found you again. You were a little more gaunt and a little more gray, but still you had that sweet and dizzy light in your aura. If I expected you to look up from the same Pessoa paperback I'd always seen in your canvas bag, that isn't how it went at all. Later you told me you hadn't read, or written, a word for eleven years. It killed something inside me, even more than your long absence. But in that moment, I forgot everything I'd imagined and saw you watching the entrance as if you were watching for me. I couldn't help falling backwards, back through all those decades, to how you almost took me on the floor, and then didn't, and then you never did. I was unbridled and lathered and bruised blue, and made myself an offering to you. Every love I made after that was overshadowed by the moment of abandoned abandon, even if I was the one who got away.

The Shawarma King

after *Kebab Chef*, Harumi Kiyota (Japan) contemporary

His hands are oddly long and whiz past fast, all whir and blur in motion. He is a cartoon, or a machine. Bird hands, as long and lean as Giacometti. He plucks plump and briny olives, coaxes fuchsia radishes onto pita. Shakes the vinegar peppers and garlic onto the meat. Drizzle, sizzle, sumac, salt. Perfection, best in show. Messy, juicy, chile afterglow. This man from Gaza. His hair is razed half an inch from his head, as if he hates an errant strand in his eyes because he can't see what's in front of him. He will not be slowed. He can craft five shawarmas at once, in five minutes flat and still superb. You have tried making small talk, asking about the world he came from. But he has fish to fry and lentils to ladle. He is always in a hurry. Even so, you have tried to convey what this means to you, having the world's best shawarma on your block, right here in Canada, next to Tim Hortons. The tahini alone is miraculous. You leave a tip the size of the sandwich, and he finally pauses, flashes a toothy smile. The man with the fast hands and the tender meat that sends you says, *well, what can I say, eh? I'm the shawarma king, I can do anything.*

white

after *Figures in a Landscape,* Bertram Brooker (Canada) 1931

marshmallows / the salt sands of bolivia / swan lake matinee / ski bunnies / magritte's bells / the holy spirit / antarctica / white gold / birch groves / vintage fox shrug / michael's glove / yuki-onago / beluga / milk of magnesia / pinprick stars/ virgen blanca (our lady of the snows) / alba de satigny / lily of the valley / simon cowell's teeth / fior di latte gelato / a dozen eggs / Bernini / spider mums / carnations / round slice of moon / glass chess/ wonder bread / cemetery markers / marilyn / marilyn's famous dress / ice storms / jackie's pearls / and coco's / sweet little lies / volterra's vases / a christmas dream / the sacrificial lamb / white chocolate / winter on the prairies / silky underwear / diana's wedding gown/ conflict free diamonds / dostoevsky in st. petersburg / cocaine blues / glenn gould's piano keys / crème fraiche / one of malevich's compositions / nights in white satin / baby powder / rice pudding / casper / ursus maritimus / sun-bleached bones / little fluffy clouds

The Peanut Butter Yarmulke

after *Chocolate Peanut Butter Cup Candy*, Toni Rubino (USA) contemporary

My Dad admitted it, readily, cheerfully. That he'd been praying for me, that the Lord would send a nice Jewish boy. Couldn't you have been more specific? I bawled at him, and at God, holding you up in the door-well by the scruff. You calmly removed your glasses and polished them while I ranted and raved, then reached for mine and went at them with your hankie. Dad was getting more gray by the day. He was almost translucent. But he loved for us to crank up the bed and fluff his pillows so he could join, asked for a plastic tumbler full of ice and a few fingers of white wine if it was after five. He had a birdfeeder set up right outside, told us if the window wasn't there, he would shoot the grackles and the squirrels that took everything from the hummingbirds he was luring. The dreaded grackle was staring in at us just then, all tut-tut bravado and beady insolence. Dad was patting the sheet beside him for us to join him on the bed, reached for his wine and for his Bible. You turned on your phone to record his faltering recitation, and I would thank you for that later when he was gone. But right then I was too busy pressing Reese's peanut butter cup wrappers to your shiny pate. Look, Dad, it's his yarmulke! I pointed, and we all laughed. I was thinking about licking the sugar from your skull and I know you felt my pulse quicken. I marveled how your teeth arched white right back into the gum, where mine were grimy yellow hollows from too many years of cigarettes. Dad never laid in on me about settling down, discreetly held his regrets and hopes for me close to his skin and never imposed them. I was just happy he could see me carrying on and laughing with you. I took that, even if I didn't know if we were forever, or what that even meant. Never held anything this long without breaking it.

Simon Says

after Maxime André Taccardi

Three times he says it: everybody down, everybody down, everybody down. He has a gun in one hand, and a gun in the other. We do what we are told. Slide from our seats and bow, face to the linoleum as if we are praying. Some of us are. I noticed him outside, on my way to class. He was smoking a cigarette methodically, eyes boring holes through the students walking past. He is a grade or two above me. Today there was something that set him apart, something enigmatic and magnetic. I didn't understand it, but I felt it. A frantic electricity, a voltage leaping off of him that crackled in the morning frost. Simon says, I smell piss. His hiss of disgust is for a moment the only thing in the room, then, too, the slow awful swish of his Converse down the aisles. A whimper from a girl, then a bang. Now I smell blood, Simon says. I see the gore-splattered fronds of his Levis slink past. There is a sickly whiff of something humid and flowery, and a mouth full of pennies. Bile rises in my throat when I realize it is the spoor of his first victim. We can talk about this, a voice creaks from the back. Shut up, damn it! someone else shouts. My heart is beating so fast I wonder if it will give out. I think, we don't need to talk, we need someone else with a fucking gun. Simon raps on a desk with the barrel of his upper hand. Talking in class would be uncouth, he says, deliberating each word, tapping one of his guns again against the hard surface. There is another blast and the blackboard explodes. Then pop, pop, pop, and someone starts to scream. I leave my body for a moment, watch cops stride across my mother's tidy lawn. Push the bell, call her ma'am. I feel her world turn silent. The scene changes. Now I'm in a bare room at the precinct. They've armed the survivors with hot chocolate. They speak in warm tones as we give our statements. Was there anything suspicious in his behaviour that you remember? one asks. Not really, I tell them. I didn't really know him. Who wants to be next? Simon says. Then, a sadistic giggle. What do you want from us? someone cries. Bang, bang. Sirens now, racing close, and I wonder how this is going to end. Open your eyes! he orders. Look at me! We see him now, a pistol at each temple. Just before the big bang: *I want you to know who I am,* Simon says.

Salt

after *Untitled (Blue and Grey),* Mark Rothko (USA, b. Latvia) 1963

In the dream, you have wandered into the sea. You walk on the waves as if on blue-white sands of salt in Bolivia, as if on glass stairs. You disappear into the crease where the horizon slips into the underworld, reappear sleeping beside a rusty anchor and the remains of a rowboat. The moon bends to your face, waits until your eyes flutter open to see sirens swimming away. A strange lady on a fish-net ladder stands in wait, and disappears at the moment you see her. You will eventually awaken, find your way home. But you will forever after long for the ocean. The blue will always keep you, it will feed you, it will be your most tender lover.

The Nowhere Man

after *The Nowhere Man,* Lorette C. Luzajic (Canada) 2010

He disappears into morning, slipping under the sky with a quicksilver nudge of a pointed boot. Down he dives, into the dark and deep outside of now. He leaves you three silver shells in a pale glass bowl with claws for a pedestal, a scattering of fox nails, and petals from dried flowers. What would you see if you could see me? he asked you, day before yesterday, day before ever. You saw a hole and a mirror, a rip in the world. Nothing, you told him out loud, tipping your littlest finger to your blindfold.

The Land of Wind and Ghosts

after *Archaeological Reminiscence of Millet's Angelus,* Salvador Dali (Spain) 1934

Before I find my way back to myself, the earth is molten and red. Fiery rocks tumble in exaggerated motion, as if in comic book art. Rips through the ground zig zag and tear with an intensity and animation that feels cosmic. There are black birds in a long row, way, way up in the distant sky, at the end of a telephone pole that teeters into eternity.

I have been gone for years, days, hours, and I land hard right where I left myself, stretched out on the grass under the willow tree next to my brother. I hear a vacant and raucous cackle, forced laughter, following me from the underworld, and wonder briefly what it's all about before realizing it is my own voice. I snap into place with a pop, shake my head.

My brother has a finger on his stop-watch. Five minutes and forty seven seconds, he says.

It's his turn next. He takes the pipe, holds the palm of his hand out and offers up the plant he's about to burn to the open sky. I'm still shell shocked, almost want to hold him back from that place. But I spark the torch and hold it under the bowl of *salvia divinorum.* Diviner's sage.

He has told me the stories of the Mazatec people around Oaxaca, Mexico, where the plant grows, how they use it in traditional spiritual rites. They call it *La Maria.*

After several inhales, the kit spills onto the lawn and he slumps against the trunk. His hand on his knee spasms a bit, then fingers splay out calm. His pinkie ring is gold, and the next one is our late father's, a gift from the factory on his retirement. The ring on his index finger is an antique compass.

Where he is now, a compass is useless.

It was transcendence I was after, but even more, disintegration. There was no shortage of tinctures and potions in my curiosity cabinet with this alchemical pursuit in mind. My brother was more selective, reserving his altered states for sacred plants and eschewing my favourite poisons.

His understanding of fate and faith was somewhat shamanic. I just wanted to jump.

I watch him flicker back into his body, the way I watched him push against our mother's belly once, wanting out. He sputters, eyes darting to and fro under his lids just like during REM. Then he lands, back in this place, returning to my side.

I knew he would be fine, but I'm still relieved. He is all I have. We are all that is left of our fractured family.

Five minutes, twenty-two seconds, I count. We had read about the suspension of time under the sage's influence, planned to measure it in earthly units and compare notes with our perception or experience.

He tries to tell me what he saw. Everything was round, but in shards, he says.

I saw them, too, diamond shavings, only they were glowing embers, intricate crystal layers from inside the core of the earth itself. They were bubbles of fire.

Did you see the birds? I ask. There are tears streaming down his face, as empty and hard as my hollow laughter. He considers it for a moment. Maybe, he says. All I can remember is how the place felt. It was the land of wind and ghosts.

He stands up, wavers a bit, brushes grass from denim. It was beautiful and terrible, he says. It was like the eye of the storm.

No, he says, thinking again. Not a storm. It was like the eye of the apocalypse.

He takes my hand, yanks me up. We walk up the stone laneway, past the pond and the chicken coop and the inukshuk sentinels. I didn't know the world we'd just gone to and returned from, but his words were everything. *The eye of the apocalypse.* That was exactly what we had always been to each other.

Soppressata

after *The Sausage Maker,* David Teniers the younger (Belgium) 1650

Luigi is talking. He is almost a hundred, and might make it there. Listen, he says. This. How soppressata is made. He spears some slices, slippery with fat, with a toothpick and passes them around. First, boil the pig-head for a few hours. Use the best meat, including the tongue. The casing must be wide and squat, not cylindrical, and traditionally flattened between two planks. The best soppressata is born from thriftiness and gratitude to fallen beast- leaving no waste to spoil. Regional spices differ. Garlic and cloves may be crushed under mortar and pestle. Salt is key. Peppercorns are king. Spicy versions are popular, with intense chiles permeating the meat. You can flavour the fat with nutmeg and juniper berries, like gin. *Salumi* does not just mean salami, he explains. There is this, there is cotechino, there is prosciutto, there is nduja. You will need crusty bread and chunky olives and Roma tomatoes and gherkins. You will need wine. Luigi watches us chew, pours out more from a taverna decanter. He grew the grapes himself, fed them to ferment, and to the pigs we are now eating. He has never heard of vegans, or the word charcuterie.

Sunday Bloody Sunday

after *Bullfight,* Elaine de Kooning (USA) 1959

The humidity was relentless, and the throngs were intimidating. I wanted to run, but the whole thing was my idea. I wanted to go to a bull fight before they were outlawed from history. I was a former vegetarian with a squeamish side, but also a thing for intense experiences. I had to. It was a Sunday in Lima. Naively, I expected to be a rare woman there, enlisted two men to accompany me. But it was an event where revelers went to see and be seen, and the women in their finest screamed the loudest for the blood.

My spare Spanish was enough to get the gist, but the macabre ballet transcended language and I let the choreography of the oldest story take me onto its plane. The gamut of emotions was an initiation I had braced for: I knew I was entering into deep mythology, attending a spectacle where the borders of life and death were under ritual enactment. Once I'd asked my husband why he loved boxing the most of all sports, and he said, because it's a real fight, not a game. The whole fight club ethos had never been appealing, but his honesty made me understand the draw. The game that's not a game. The bullfight was, still, this. More than all the drama and fanfare and the crowds, it was all about going through right to the end. Not the edge of it, not just theatre, but to the intersection of life and death, and past it. Going all the way there. Until one was fallen.

My first response was a feminist one. How the great warrior sent to battle and overcome nature was actually feminine. It was all elegant calisthenic, lime green satin, sleek, slender, tender, slippered. Velvet and glitter. My second emotion was an endless sadness, watching the tamed beast dragged around and around the track, trailing blood, while the crowd lust roared wild in the searing Sunday sun.

That matador, victorious. The best outcome, of course, although the alternative was a roulette he had consensually courted. Even so, to witness the goring of this young, effete toreador would have scarred me for life, even as I'd paid those pesos for my ticket to chance it.

We walked for miles, afterward, looking for a cab. Couldn't quite believe what we'd just witnessed. That defeat, that fallen beast, the myth and the strange power of it, the pyramids crashing down to silence.

Rapture

after *The Last Judgement,* Michelangelo (Italy) 1541

The last time I saw Bobby, I watched him clap his hands together in church as if he hadn't just been doing time. As if his days weren't numbered, as if the pipe would not return before four more moons. I was off of the hard shit myself, for good but didn't know it yet: we went back so many times. I heard him sing "This Little Light of Mine" and move those slim dungaree hips like Aretha Franklin, the hardened con in him melting in God's glow. He was a dead man walking. I might have even guessed it, and I guess I already had, I already knew, but for that moment, I was in the rapture and not thinking of what was coming after. I asked the spirit to make me oblivious, just for that hour. There was a thunder of black hooves, and white stallions, and the choir behind them. The piano pounded fortissimo praise at the rafters. There was a light on Bobby's face that I'll never forget, as if that promise of redemption was a real possibility. It gave me hope I shouldn't have had, hope I hold onto still in the quietest, farthest reach of me. That Bobby wouldn't die alone, even though he did.

The Wishing Machine

after *The Magic Circle,* John William Waterhouse (UK) 1886

You are afraid of sleeping in a room that isn't yours. It is why you can't sleep deep enough for renewal; your mind grasps for familiar markers as you drift and toss. You keep the laptop on for blue light, to see the outlines of your world when you stir or shift. There are other small terrors in your treasury of memory, and in bundles you have yet to open. There is a rusty key with a thin red ribbon, and a shrivelled monkey's paw, bound in bloody silk. There is a box within a box within a box, and a sachet of petals and crushed glass. The spindle, the crank and rattle, the medley of small seeds. But the worst of the curses that surround you is her psionics device. With its nifty dials and intricate web of wires, it could almost be proudly displayed, a beautiful curiosity, at a museum of invention or intention gone wrong, an oddity in the dustbins of science. But it is a ball and chain. It is a thing that cannot be put aside or buried. You can't leave it behind: it must be passed on to someone you deem worthy. *Be careful what you wish for* is the oldest lesson in story-time and psych, never mind all those smug mottos about manifestation and vibrations. So you simply won't hand it off, give another the curse of their desires. The deception of it all surrounds you, keeps you from action, from what you know is the only honest way of making a life out of life. You floated into this world of spells and signs on the salt waves of a woman who promised you would inherit her gifts. It was a poison you can't shake off. You were woven out of her. If only she had spent less time baying at the moon and wiggling her fingers in the aura glow of dead ancestors, she might have seen how much you wanted to partake in the here and now, to join the living. Instead you are still shivering, you are easily startled, and you haven't slept in years.

The White Room

after *White on White,* Kazimir Malevich (Russia) 1918

Wordsworth in winter. The psalmody in sunlight. Dylan, not yet gone, Dylan, not yet born. She is turning pages. She is caught on the white slant of summer's last light, biding rhyme. On another continent, the blues are being born.

Sweet and Sour

after *Calvin and Hobbes,* Bill Watterson (USA)1985-1995

We choke down the liver and onions with hot sauce and lime, all because I keep mumbling about Vitamin A. While you are airing out the fragrance of entrails, I am scrabbling under your bed for the Calvin and Hobbes compendium I kicked out the way last night when we were getting nasty on the floor. Your thighs were solid rocks against the puffy expanse of my menopausal belly. You are as bald as an eagle and I was a hangry hawk: we were urgent and comical. I find what I'm looking for, spread the cartoon strip open, wait for you to join me before finally laughing out loud solo. You amble in with yellow gloves to your elbows and Tiger King undies, to see what's so funny, but I've already gone under. You pull the white sheets over me if I'm already dead. *Me Calvin, you Jane,* you say, hurling Hobbes aside when you climb in beside me, dishes done and gone. I stir somewhere inside of nine o'clock and fifty, tell you to do it again.

Twitter

after *The Twittering Machine,* Paul Klee (Switzerland) 1922

Tweet, tweet, twitter, twitter, all those stunning and brave flags. Brevity is the source of all wit, so said the bard, but maybe he was wrong. The nattering of the concise and irate, condensed outrage, this incessant twittering in the wings, so ubiquitous that it is almost white noise. So much is brittle and huffy and mean. We want so desperately to publicly separate ourselves from sinners, that we fail to see we have become witch hunters, pointing the same fingers, setting the same fires. We are a swarm of gossiping birds, a murder of karens.

Horoscope

after *The Stroll,* Gertrude Abercrombie (USA) 1943

The past is always with us, it is written overhead in the stars. They are wrong when they say you can see the future in the Milky Way - it is everything before us that is still knit by the darkness. Each sapphire prick through the cloak of night is long gone. Well, once I talked to a man who saw a man who left no footprints in the snow. It was a deep and cold Wednesday and he saw a strange silence stumbling through the woods in oddly patterned vestments. Wouldn't have thought anything of it save the fact he hadn't seen a soul outside for days. He was as there and as real as the warm bullet he once plucked a metre from his prey during the war. Once I talked to my grandmother about how she had answered the door to him the night before her son was disassembled by a train, four thousand miles away. I have my own ghosts, too, small scars between witness and belief. I spent some of my future chasing them backwards, but no more. There's too much tangled in the done and gone. The now and not yet is a mystery, a story we are still writing.

I Hope You Are Wrong

after *Hypnosis,* Claude Tousignant (Canada) 1956

I hope you are wrong, but I fear you are right, my friend said. She picked at something on the checkered gabardine of her lapel with great focus.

I had shared my view that the Chauvin trial verdict would end in flames no matter what it was. It was seldom my way to talk with anyone about all that went on in my mind, preferring to observe the world around me. But I had a long-time and unique bond with my friend and enjoyed being able to talk nuance and hear honest and conflicting ideas.

In any event, we both had mutual acquaintances in the vicinity, and they had already vacated, as if they had been warned of a typhoon, as if the forest on fire was already there in the city centre, and of course, it was.

People say it is black and white, my friend said, but it isn't. She had moved on to the scrutiny of a ring finger hangnail. It's not that way at all. It is gray and yellow.

I was really trying to understand what she was nervously trying to convey, meaning to listen carefully, but my mind jumped immediately to a giant Tousignant print we'd once had in the foyer.

It was a minimalist affair in just those colours, all pristine geometrics: a slim stripe of daffodil yellow beside a rectangle pool of fresh paved asphalt. I'm not sure now where the thing came from. It was faded and framed cheaply in utilitarian plastic, possibly left over from the tenants before us. Even so, I liked it.

I was always drawn to more complicated paintings, with many layers and a variety of motivating factors that figured into the big picture.

But the contrast in Claude's colours was perfection: the tidy veneer over the dark void of our human soul on the one hand, the purifying pale fire on the other.

Wild Things

after *Centauress,* John La Farge (USA) 1887

1. You had my heart bad, Bobby. You had it, held it, broke it. Oh, I knew it. I was under no illusions by then about my strange penchants and the trouble they always bring me. You were hesitant, almost sweet, the first time we made love. Touched me so tenderly, looked at me for so long, I knew I'd never get away.

2. Only after he had gone did it dawn on me- how much that cat looked like Elvis. He was ridiculously good looking, but also looked ridiculous. Spencer was baby-faced, almost fat, and his eyes had the devil in them. But none of that was why you wanted him so fiercely. It was something else, some broken, lost thing. The thing you fell for every time.

3. At the round glass table, after a few repeat fingers of rum, Lance tells me about Borneo. His stint as a sniper. I've heard a lot of Lance's stories, huddled on the bed under his mother's crochet. The year in jail, or the time the Indians made him an honorary member of their tribe. About all those lost ones he saved from the brink of jumping, just by showing up. Me, too- maybe you could say that. Lance never talks about the military. But he has turned 77, on a borrowed ankle, hip, and knees. He wants us to know something about what happened. How evil changes you. How the shit you see fucks you up forever. How once, painted green and mud, shrouded by matching leaves, he came face to face with the enemy, brown man, white man, gun to gun in the jungle.

How Lance put his finger to his lips and caught the soldier's eye. How they both backed down and got away.

4. On my wedding day, cutting lines with the sailor I had known just a few weeks. Our hearts were beating madly. The enormity of the thing was upon us. I was exhausted and elated. Truth be told, I'd been waiting for something wild to happen. I was craving it with the core of my sickness, and maybe even also the best parts in me. Talked to the goddess from a broken toilet seat at a bar, heard her siren lute pure and clear over the live grunge reverb shaking the stalls. And now, here I was. We were as close as two souls could be, it was that fast. But here I was. The beautiful taste of melting white plastic, the chemical sting in the drip. I barely had you, but already right then, I let you go inside my mind. I was terrified, too, knew, this time I had really jumped.

5. Mr. Brown entered my psyche in eighth grade, in a vortex of rumours of weapons, of chemical explosives in his locker. He was a jaunty little thing, defiant, defensive, clever af. Could already sweet talk his way out of anything, but seldom talked at all. By the middle of secondary art history, I understood that still waters ran deep. Borrowed his *Demian,* Hesse, lent him Leonard Cohen, gave him my Dosteoevsky. Sometimes in the morning, years after we'd lost touch and before we found it again, I would wake up from dreaming. I was sure I'd been talking to him out loud, wherever he was.

6. Rob is a kind of miner and archeologist. He talks to arrowheads and silver. He chars myrrh in a cauldron on his stone table, examines specimens under flickering kerosene.

A tooth, maybe, or a button a century asunder from a soldier's coat. Once, I held a bullet he had found in the creek under a cave, fingered the sluiced grooves in the metal. When I asked if his shovel had injured his find to make those marks, he shook his head, held the round to the flame. You've heard the phrase, bite the bullet, he said. Think about what it might mean. And just like that, he conjured that for me, a man's agony across the years right here in our backyard, in a world before anesthesia or morphine. Amputations, surgeries in wartime, with nothing but brandy and a steel marble between your molars. We lock eyes in the jittering shadows from the fire. Rob nods, turns back to the hide he is beading at the table. He was like that, my brother, he could see everything, all the things, all the ones, who had been here already.

7. J. was a software programmer and engineer before such things existed. He could also belt out an aria or a chorus of gospel right up there with Mahalia, or Michael, a voice like a clarinet or a brook. He had a white cockatiel that went with him on his paper delivery routes. He tried to explain the binary codes to me, how everything there was, was made of ones and zeros. He would set off a cacophony of sound on the dot matrix, reel off a few sheets to show me the endless sequencing of slim lines and circles. By thirteen, he was trying to explain to me how they were tracking us. Point to the traffic lights which held secret files on all things we had done. He caked his face with stage makeup, powdered his acne with a kabuki brush. Used it to dust the floorboards for bugs and wires. He had a dozen cats. Wore patent black witch boots and yellow tights to the office. Was a chess whiz

and read dozens of beautiful slender books of poetry. Gone by thirty, another red ribbon casualty. I can still hear his laughter, and all that terrible silence.

8. My first true love was a prophet, Malachi, the last book of the Old Testament. His face was wide and dark and scars zig zagged over his black body. He was the jester, always too loud, too funny, too eager for centre stage. He would break dance in Jackson Square, perform contortions in the Georgia diner, eagerly hawk jejune hip-hop poetry to anyone he could overwhelm. I left him in Houston and tried to go all the way to Vancouver, couldn't get him out of my mind. Ran back, tried to find him. We were rebels without a clue. I slept against his beating heart in the ruins of a burnt down, abandoned plantation house on the Esplanade in New Orleans. He battled vampires for me, warded off the gutter punks tripped out on cough syrup and self-disgust. When I hovered over him behind the dumpster in Texas, I didn't think I could ever come back from the spell I was under. The skies that night- there have never been so many stars.

9. I was nine, I was sleuthing the woods for murder, for salamanders and haunts. Near to our cottage, there was an old sea captain living in a shed in the woods. My father took me to find him. I had Dorothy Hamill hair and my breasts were small mosquito bites, puffy nubs about to ignite. My daughter, Dad said, presenting me to the silver-tressed man who had shyly emerged from a log cabin. I stood in drooling stupor before a grimy cabinet of old medals and buttons. There were animal skins hanging behind us, and snowshoes, and ropes of drying berries. There were rusty things and

antlers on his table. He reminded me of my brother, but I didn't know that yet. Robert would not yet come to us for another five winters.

10. Thirty years after she was slain like a lamb a mile from where I ended up living, Elaine is still like oxygen, still a winding wound through my innocence. I can smell her perfume. She rushes up in that cloud of smoke and powdery Vanderbilt. The way it clung, sweet like a bee, to the earth and musk of her leather. I was always trying to bring Bee to Jesus, tried to sell her on the social justice angle. I thought she was courage incarnate, spiked and bleached and stapled, and always headed to the city to hold up her signs for something or other. One time, she didn't come home. I didn't think anything of it until the cops called, asked a few questions I didn't have answers to. Then, saw her smile from the cover of a tabloid. *Charred Remains.* Raped by four anarchist thugs, strangled after the protest against capital punishment. I still had a note she had passed me in grade ten math class, still have it now. *I'd rather be standing in front of an oncoming Mac truck than sitting here...* Murder, she wrote.

11. Well, if I always saw myself sleek and twisty, dusky mirrored and soaked in Byron and sea fog, in green brocade and red velvet, to some drumbeat heartbeat, that was just the Romantic streak in my blood. It was part true and part lie, like everything we perceive. I was an Amazon, a musketeer, the girl on the threshold, Nancy Drew, Harriet the Spy, Alice, and the cat with wings. I was ready to step inside the space craft and take flight to another world. Popped every

pill, hitched every ride. I was chasing after horses and sinking ships, dreaming of diamonds and caravans. I still wander those fields of glory with my scissors and my pen, shunting my rifle at all my predators and ghosts. We are all gypsies, aren't we? Wild things, starving for love and stories, for the sea and the wind and the dawn.

Fifteen Shades of Gray

after *Abstract Painting*, Gerhardt Richter (Germany) 2000

Here are the smudges and the signs, all that you have asked of me. Here they are, every imprint of cheesecloth and nails, every cut of the claw. I have nothing else to give you, no sage sight, no terrible and beautiful words. I have no ahas and no epiphanies, no wit or wonder. It is a handful of screws and hinges, a medley of metal and wire. It is how you asked me to show up, frightened and naked and ready to jump.

Disco Nefertiti

after Amedeo Modigliani

for Garfunkel

You asked about Marie and I didn't know what to tell you. I'd last seen her wedged atop my bookshelves, her sly smile up there blank and all knowing, and it hadn't dawned on me until that moment that I hadn't seen her for some time. Marie, the long-necked Madonna of disco. I would have guessed her sultry vintage stare was painted on just as Abba hit their stride, but she was as aloof and flawless as Nefertiti, another incarnation. Nah, you said when you gifted her to me- she's a real redhead, like me. I had to agree and ended up spray painting her russet when she got dusty. I heaped her in swathes of little disco balls that bloomed pink and baby blue when the last light fell through the blinds. Her neck grew as long as our friendship. Once you strapped Marie to the front of your boyfriend's Bronco, and she rode unblinking through Wyoming and Michigan to land back home. When you left again you placed her at the topmost shelf in my library and she'd never gone anywhere since. How long had it been since Marie's discreet disappearance and now? I had no idea where she'd gone or who had taken her. Sometimes it's like that, a small mystery, like how the day I met you, you were long and thin and orange like the cat I loved who had fallen fatally from the balcony that very morning. I named you after him, a moniker you wore from then on forward. We never agreed on anything but "Suzanne" by Leonard Cohen, thrift store oddities, and New Orleans. It didn't matter, nothing did, in that kind of friendship, easy as Sunday morning.

Mr. Jones

after found thrift-store painting of man peeling potatoes, artist not known

Mr. Jones is sick of solanine: by now, craggy spurs and creaky knuckles from the dark bursting eyes of his spuds are weary nuisances. Still he pares on, with Saint at his side. The room's musk of dog and potatoes is a hallmark after all these years. Sometimes they'll both be rattled from reverie by the racket of teacups when the train rumbles past behind them. Mr. Jones might put his knife aside, summon Saint to the backyard for a sniff and a woof among earthworms and the falling night. He might light a pipe for a few swift puffs, stub out the nest of tobacco with the tip of his finger when he turns in. The whistle way off sounds like a song he used to know.

The Neon Raven

after *Nightfall,* Will Barnet (USA) 1979

"For Goddesses may be as qualmish as Gipses…"
Bacchinalia Coelestia: A Poem in Praise of Punch,
Alexander Radcliffe

I noticed her right away- you'd have to be dead not to.

Branwenn was a barely contained meteor, electric, neon, buzzing and sparking under all that funerary frippery she was buried in. All black in blazing colours. A raven raining rainbows. She wouldn't have noticed me at all if I'd been wearing another T-shirt, but she did notice me. *I want that,* she said simply, wagging a few dozen rings at my cleavage. The word "damaged" was embroidered across my chest in tiny yellow flowers. Her eyes were dark holes and I fell into them on my way to the bar.

What could I do?

I asked the bartender to pour me twice as much and offered her a straw.

Before the glass was empty, we were kissing and her rings were skimming my breasts and nape and the small of my back under my jeans. I wanted it to be enough, but I went home with head pounding, wanting more.

She wasn't hard to get and she wasn't easy: it's just that she was almost not there, even in the beginning when we couldn't keep our hands off of each other. I could never quite reach her or find my way inside. She told me about it before she ever stayed over. *I've never really loved anybody,* she said, *not really.*

I didn't believe her.

And maybe she wouldn't have told me about Crow at all if I hadn't found the small urn in her sock drawer when I meant to stow away a stack of freshly laundered thongs. I didn't know what it was, and it seemed out of place so I moved it. It could have been a stash box for pot or hold some sort of memento from a past flame. I didn't open it and did not know, but when Branwenn came back and saw it sitting on the table with a stack of library books destined for return, I couldn't read what I saw on her face. Her hand reached to snatch the box even before our eyes met. *What were you looking for?* she asked, her face narrowing, and something still fragile dissolved there. *Nothing,* I said. I pulled back. From her expression, I was expecting some kind of paranoid tirade or rage and was about to call her out on how sick I was already of walking on eggshells. Instead, Branwenn crumpled. I took her into my arms and held her up while she wept.

It was a long time before she told me what was in the box. *It's Crow,* she said finally. *He was born ten years after I was. I used to pretend I was the mother bird, is that strange?*

It is difficult to compete with the dead. She wouldn't say much more, and I didn't ask. Car crash, murder? I felt like an intruder and didn't want to pry.

I couldn't get anything right with Branwenn, it seemed. I hoped to hold her in supportive silence, not take more than she wanted to give. But she looked up after awhile and asked, *Don't you even care? Don't you even want to know?*

I'd never had much experience juggling anyone's grief but my own. I didn't want to be there. But I held the course. Perhaps it was because I cared- that's what I thought then. But there was a part of me too that wanted to gather injuries, make note of them in case I would need them later.

One day we were dancing in slutty stockings we'd found in the sale bin, scooping teacups of punch we'd made from some gin and lemons at the market. Watching her feathery fluster, her sensual and awkward groove, I wanted her more than I'd ever wanted anything at all. I wanted to spend my life with her. I wanted to give my life for her. I was spinning a little from the lust and the booze, from the magnitude of my surrender.

When I asked for a glass of water, pushed my punch back on the table, she touched my face with those soft hands and said, *Even goddesses may be as qualmish as gypsies.* I assumed she was quoting some of the strange, old fashioned poetry she loved. And just as I was about to take the plunge, fumble for the tiny diamond in my pocket, I noticed that she was far away again, and I hesitated.

And that's where things were when she said it.

You kind of look like him, Robin, do you see it? And she held a little mirror up to my face so I could see myself disappearing.

I fell back from her, furious. *You won't let me love you,* I said, finally, instead of what I'd been planning, *because you're still married to your brother.*

Maybe I had waited for a long time to say it. But if I thought I would feel liberation after getting that off my chest, wake her or shake her out of a trance with my insightful revelation, it wasn't like that at all. It was something she already knew and carried, a cage of shame along with all that grief. *You wouldn't let me love you because you knew I would betray you one day,* I thought later, the way that I did just then, the way I always turned on everything. And that was how we left it, because there was nowhere else to go after that.

Rocket Man

after *The Great Wave,* Katsushika Hokusai (Japan) 1831

I said my goodbyes, turned back to the shore, stopped trying to find you. It took me awhile, took me a few more pink striped skies, a few more mountains, a few more years. But I found my way, wrested my skin from yours, saved myself from going under. I talk to you still, the way we always talked, close and deep without platitudes or pretense. You know I have forgiven you for all the ways you almost took me with you. You didn't mean to, never meant for me to get swept into your undertow. You tried to stop it but I was desperate for a reason to fade away. Wanted someone to blame for my disappearance. But that's not how it was for us, two people too honest for games. We stood naked in our presence and our absence. The day they carried you down the stairs and later, into the oven, I still belonged to you. I belong to you still. You had already told me that where you were going I was not yet and could not be. It took me some time before I believed you, but now I do. I am here and you are there. You are, through me, and I am, through that dark mirror of soon and never. I see the stars and the planets stretch out between us, feel the worlds fall down like rain.

Our Daily Bread

after *Tarde de Verano,* Jose Basso (Chile) contemporary

The prairies are inside you, you are covered in dust and disarray, in clouds so close they are kissing the hay. The mares are tough and determined, like you, and resigned to their purpose. Well, I have always been a city mouse, even though I was born of the same bread. I wanted pavement and paintings, I wanted frosty tumblers of patio gin with crushed mint. I wanted red high heels and Barcelona. To each their own, you said, when I invited you to the city. I wanted to show you the museums and the world, but you said the whole world was under the dust right where you were. I was an old woman before I felt that kind of certainty and safety. That sense of where I stood. And if I gave a few portraits and poems to this planet, you gave us hefty, rustic loaves and cold beer. You cajoled the very earth to ignite on our behalf, to feed us.

The Narcissists

after Patrick Nagel

1. We cover our scars in scarlet, all of us. We are lean and long and carmine, like flamingos. One swipe of the lippy, smear like a gash. We are all wound. We are haute couture stick figure skeletons. Red devils. We are all eyes, holes.

2. Teeter totter Gaga spikes. Rose red kid soft leather from Italy. Thigh high. I command the room. I was playing *Truth or Dare* like Madonna and her dancers in these same boots. Someone asked about the meanest thing you ever did. I said nothing, but my mind went instantly back, to an earlier place wielding this same power. My little brother is blue, and trembling, from too long in the ice-cold lake. I wrap him in a warm towel and press him against my big new breasts. He is twelve. *Want to see them?* I whispered it so softly that no one else has ever heard me.

3. You drive past the gallery wearing a PVC harness dress. Then swoop back. You can't stand him in the limelight, or anyone else, really. You storm inside, disrupting the artist's story over Chenin Blanc and Brie because it's all about you. It's only ever been about you. You wanted so desperately to be famous, but now it's happening to somebody else. Someone you once called a friend. You want him to stop everything when he sees you, to tremble, to acquiesce his platform to its rightful owner. He laughs. He knows what you are. He remembers everything. You hate to be mocked.

You are seething. He is still laughing. *Lord,* he says. Out loud, in front of everyone. *You haven't changed a bit.*

4. In a fugue, the young woman marched to the rooftop. *See me*, she said, to anyone watching on Instagram. Stepped off, fell down, sundown, long gone. Without the camera, she doesn't even exist. She is varnish, shell, shellac. All surface, all illusion. She hasn't eaten for days, maybe weeks. She wants to watch herself bleed. Witness them fussing around her beautiful corpse on the ground. Her last thought is not, oh, God, what have I done, but OMG, how will I see myself disappearing?

5. We drape ourselves in red velvet, claw scattered stars with lacquered talons. We accuse those we used to love of unspeakable crimes, just to watch their lives crumble under the force of our lies. We crisscross our cuts, ram our fingers down our throat, drown our babies in bathtubs. We like it when you watch.

The Mists of Catalan

after *View of Barcelona from a Rooftop in Riera de Sant Joan,* Ramon Marti i Alsina (Spain) 1889

On our last day in Barcelona, we watched the rain from the palace museum of art, over Catalonia. If I'd dreamed of dashing in and out of cathedrals to make love for days, now I was so tired I wasn't sure I'd make it to Madrid. Our bed was two small boards and a bit of foam pushed together, but our aching knees were grateful even so. Falling into you, yielding to you, for the thousandth time, after so many mosaics and so much serrano ham, was a kind of baptism, or medicine. It never escaped me how lucky I was. Your company was easy and I was heavy, but you carried me like air. You braced my elbow, held my neck in the bend of your arm, packed up all my what-ifs in a suitcase with wheels. When I was drowning in all the graves and poems, you tied a crimson ribbon to my pinkie. Spain! you said, before we got there, when I was still afraid, waving the word like a fuchsia frock in front of a bull, then wiping my tears with the stars spilling over the hillside, gathering me in that crook like a shepherd.

Downpour

after *Waiting (145)*, Brett Amory (USA) contemporary

We weren't expecting the downpour, but an umbrella would have been useless anyways. When the sky buckled without warning, a river spilled down, and you couldn't hide your face from the gods. You were stopped by the storm, wrestling your armload of apples out of the wind. I had the window hauled open and waited for you at the cusp of the elements. I loved the torrents so much that I had a longing inside to give myself over to them. It wasn't unlike the way I interrupted your sleep and invited you to swallow me whole. I was always at the threshold of some kind of abandon, while you were out there, forsaken, ferocious, aflame. Something was always holding me down, the privilege of safety, or the illusion.

The Pink Café

after *Pink Café,* Fikret Mualla (Turkey) 1958

I didn't know what you were talking about, but you kept talking anyways. That's how you were, yappy and persistent. You had to get it out. I could have been more patient, if you'd shown some restraint. I was restless while you hung your heart out to dry, stifled some yawns, snuck a peek at my phone to see if anyone else was looking for me. Still, I stayed, and no one else did. I tell myself that counts for something when I turn everything over in my head about that night.

Night Flight

after *Tammuz,* Mordechai Ardon (Israel) 1962

Imagine, we were half bird. Our flight is fleeting, yes, but still we sometimes slipped into the sky. You are new to this world and don't know the half of it. Even so, you show us the way. How to slay the dragons, how to turn the page. We gnaw on plastic poultry legs and rubbery bananas and you fake punch a random price into a toy cash register, hold your grubby paw out for my pocketful of coins. I wouldn't have wished the world on you, but here you are. You have arrived, starry eyed and surprised. You have a blue-green bike and a matching bow in your hair. You love cucumbers and mangos and the frilliest pajamas. Every word is a victory and you're starting to string them together. We were dancing in our sock feet in your toy room, stripes and polka dots a blur in your swirl. If only we had more ice cream, you say when I pull out the goodnight story. You stall for time before lights out and I guess it's the same for all of us. *Lord, just one more year, just one more day, just one more hour.* But soon you are drifting through the clouds and I watch sleep soften your small face. The moon is your witness, I think, kissing you where she does on your dimple. I cover you in a thin sheet, watch your shifting shoulders, small wings dark as earth.

Feeling the Blues

after *Sweet Home Blue Chicago,* John Carroll Doyle (USA) 1993

His harmonica is heavy, breathe in, breathe out, harmony, cacophony, restless, breathless, bravado. I can hear the low thrumming even after I leave the bar. I don't know how to hear jazz, how to separate myself when I've left the room and the song is still soaking the whorls of my veins and my sockets. I told him I was taken after the shiraz was sent to my table, told you I was broken after the song she spun made me bleed there on the floor. I warned you of all the drama that comes with me, the sticky stories that make up a life. It was self-absorbed, and foolish, I saw in retrospect, to be so afraid I'd fail you, as if you didn't have a web of your own.

Drowned World

after *Snow Storm*, J.M.W. Turner (England) 1842

"I wished to show what such a scene was like; I got the sailors to lash me to the mast to observe it; I was lashed for four hours, and I did not expect to escape, but I felt bound to record it if I did." J.M.W. Turner

The ice is the air, a swirl of crushed sapphires and black diamonds, brutal against your face. In modern days, our only shipwreck is Rose's, epic, romantic, Titanic. But Jack does not wait in the deep here to rescue or woo, leave our unfinished symphony in grandeur and celluloid. Here, it is only God, the elements, wind and hail, swallowing a steamboat whole in the mouth of the harbour. The water is a black hole, a vortex taking you six miles under. Turner's contemporaries huffed and snorted over his frantic brushwork. They still wanted mechanical historical drafts devoid of marrow. Turner was painting something else, a self-portrait, his own fear. He is what we don't see in the painting, the artist, tied to the mast, broken to prayer. The tempest heard him, dropped him soaked and freezing, black and blue at the shore, left us with this portal into deep sea drowning.

Yahtzee

after *Card Players,* Lucas Van Leyden (Netherlands) 1525

for Ralph

Ralph is picking fruit flies from his wine, the red one that tastes like cupcakes. His weird long pinky nail is a scoop. *At least they died happy,* he says. We are in that space we love to be together, warm, and a little boozy. We laugh in each other's company more than two sad and anxious people have any right. Ralph throws his head back, turns all teeth, and his chuckle is baritone. I crack up like a little girl. Even so, I am overbearing and mothering but that's just how much I love. Once I wanted to save him from a crush and that other friend's darkness, had to pull back, let him go and find out on his own, since he was a grown man. Almost old enough to be my father. We loved to sit at the corner end of a crowded bar, slowly stewing over craft beer and Yahtzee. We would make up stories about the people around us, imagining their lives. Once, near the end of a game, I crossed out my Yahtzee. Odds were, I wouldn't need it. My next roll was five fives in one toss. That's how my luck always was, epic and useless. Ralph had his roadblocks too. The way he let things go by when he really wanted to be a part of them, the way he couldn't say no to people if he might hurt them. We commiserated over how long it had been since we'd written any good poetry, and over how long it had been since either of us had really been in love. That was how it came about, the night of the cupcakes, our creative collaboration. We were going to write a book of poems about Jennifer

Tilly! It would be called *Poker Face.* Jennifer was everything I wanted to be, the woman who would play me in my biopic. Ralph's character would be an Oscar-worthy role, of course, a performance by Anthony Hopkins or Ian McKellen. I just wanted Jennifer, quirky, with heroic cleavage, the card-shark brains behind boobs any sane woman would envy. I'd dreamed of being a chess genius when I was small, before it was apparent I wouldn't even graduate high school because of the math. Jennifer ditched her breathless brunette acting roles for the big-time world of poker championships, turning the boys to dust. Ralph took a pen in hand. We eagerly jotted down notes on our future literary masterpiece, even though it would never materialize. *Oh, Jennifer, your radiant areolas,* Ralph pined and pantomimed in the air, wriggling his hands. Then, that shock of silver tossed back, those white teeth wide. I suggested haikus about nipples. Our work on the male and female gaze would be ground-breaking, meteoric. We had many brave ideas! We would write odes to Jennifer's pale decolletage, write about Jennifer's cupid's bow. We would find old paintings about playing cards, weave them like a tapestry against stories of our most contemporary goddess. Jennifer Tilly, curvy, fifty, sharp and bubbly, bride of lucky. How I wanted to be her. How I loved Ralph most of anyone, because he said I already was. Once in Manitoba I watched Ralph tilt his camera at the sky, capture the clouds falling into the marsh where we were wandering far from the car. How he held the whole wide world inside his lens. There were times he turned his camera back on me, like when I torched all my paintings in his backyard. It was the kind liberation ceremony only Ralph would understand. *You got to know when to hold 'em, know when to fold 'em*...We never did write that book of Tilly. This is our sign of friendship: Jennifer, in a wrap dress, breasts defying gravity and time. And those soused fruit flies scattered at the side of his napkin, beside two olive pits, so happy to be drowned.

Conceal/Carry

after *The Boat (Claude Monet in His Floating Studio),* Edouard Manet (France) 1874

Everyone has small secrets, you said once when you wanted to back away from prying. I almost told you everything right then. You had a hand full of Twizzlers, ever since you quit smoking, and I watched you methodically chew one branch after another. We were dappled in sunlight, lolling gently along in a small boat. The scenery was idyllic. I didn't apologize for a delicious cigar, made a ceremony of tapping the ash onto the lights on the water. I wished that you would draw me, paint me, outline my contours in charcoal. I wanted that fleeting sense of permanence, imagined the strokes and gestures of your pencil and your brush. But you wouldn't do it. Said it would make you feel too naked. Well, there were times I almost asked you what was behind those closed doors. But I felt compelled to allow you the dignity of a mystery. When everyone else was desperately hawking their secrets to anyone online who would gasp, you were cool and contained, held the weight of whatever it was with a kind of integrity I'd never possessed myself. I somehow wanted to honour that. So I held my curiosity the way you held your secrets. And if I imagined them unravelling in the lone dark when I wasn't with you, I never told you anything about it until now.

Robin Eggs

after *Self Portrait,* Helen Lundeberg (USA) 1944

If you were waiting for the wind, you didn't tell me. You didn't talk about the slanting sun that fell over the heap of barnboards, or the flames that took all our letters. I was the one who left, so I'm the one to blame. If I got lost in the labyrinth of land mines scattered over our city, I never said so. We both knew the unspoken things, the ghosts with the long fingers. Once we watched the mist creep under the pines, shroud the pyramids we were building. We were eleven, twelve, almost thirteen. There was a broken cassette tape, heel-crushed and blooming from a thistle. There were two blue eggs, early birds like we were, still spattered and spangled, still sheltered by that calcium caul.

Eternity and Impermanence

after *Inclined Buddha Wall Painting at Weherahena, Matara,* artist and date not known (Sri Lanka)

for Jamyang Khedrup

Have you forgotten already? There were fractals of fire spinning at the centre of the well. The dark could see you coming. Your crackling light. Well, I was prone to seeing things or maybe I could just see past the veil. You glowing something ancient. Saffron frock in a sarcophagus, eternal calm. Everyone gathered around you, wanting to touch your hem. I never doubted for a minute, even if I didn't believe.

Girl at the Market

after *Market Stall,* Charles Wilda (Austria) 1906

The air is thick with burning cloves, with solanine and coriander. You are wearing the string of red coral beads I brought you in a goat skin pouch. A tagine in the souk is simmering fat forkfuls of fish and ginger, but you wave away the invitation. I scatter a few cashews among the persimmons on the table. I won't wait forever, and you won't hurry for anyone.

Quill and Quire

after *Blue Reach,* Helen Frankenthaler (USA) 1974

Think about it this way, you tell someone who sees what you see: you have been given four feathers. Two are small, sidling softly under, and two are peacock plumes with turquoise jewels for eyes. What do you keep, and what do you leave behind? Which will you dip into ink and touch to paper, wrestle with history, or with the sky? Perhaps it is not my place to ask, or to pry. You may have forgotten all the signs I gave you.

The Passenger

after *Untitled (Car Crash),* Jean Michel Basquiat (USA) c. 1980

for Elijah Newman

The driver is chatting with his youngest son on Face Time, finishing his second coffee, when a fare beeps through. Got to go, kiddo, he says, high fiving the small brown palm through the screen. Do your homework! He has a bad feeling low inside himself when he sees the teenager who climbs into the back seat. His face is sullen and hard. Elijah sees too many young boys like this- the kinds of fares who will take him on a wild goose chase just for kicks, or refuse to pay. He greets the boy, mutters a few stilted platitudes about the weather and the traffic, but the kid's hostile expression doesn't waver. They spin through the streets, and Torian's eyes bore holes in the back of Elijah's head. He says something, but Elijah can't quite hear him. Say it again? he says. This time he can hear the boy clearly, sees him waving the pistol in the rear-view mirror. Cold and tough, all video gangster. I got some money, Elijah says, trying to swallow the bile, trying not to slam into the car in front of him. I can get you some cash! The last things he thinks before the bullet pounds his chest, and then the windshield: my kid's unfinished spelling paper; how there will be no marches, no protests, for me.

Ventriloquy

after *Pandemic Evolution, Day 24*, Matthew Wolfe (USA) 2020

1. Inside the tin where rain and dead cigarettes would later pool their poisons, that's where I left your letters. If it was empty by the time you got there, who should we blame?

2. And if I usually had someone else speak for me, it wasn't always true.

3. You had your own way against words, always waiting for me to do the talking.

4. None of this matters now in our long silence. Only the rude red round wound of heart we shared is real. Can you hear me, now, in all the things I never said when I had the chance?

5. I wasn't waiting for you to save me, but I wouldn't have stopped you either.

Green Fan, Sleeping Lady

after *Unknown Title,* Nguyen Tuong Lan (Vietnam) 1942

A swarm of swallows swallows the sun; I coax the curtain just a little to let the last light fall over you. You have been reading too many haikus. Your days have grown shorter because of it.

A Wrinkle in Time

after *Woman with Checked Shirt Walking with Cane,* Bill Traylor (USA) by 1949

It is only a handful of times I have walked with a cane. I am still getting used to the mileage my kneecap has borne, to leaning on anything or anyone. We wait for the elevator, and I joke about smacking you across your ass with the swing of my stick. The doctor has told me to lose weight and take glucosamine. As we wait for the lift, I grumble about the cartilage erosion under the heft of my thigh, wonder how I'll make my way to the washroom for the next twenty years. I'm too young to be this old, I whine, but we all are, aren't we? I am wishing I was thin and tidy, not larger than life and in slow motion, with disaster after disaster following me. You take my elbow and usher me through the door. I think of our relief just this morning, when you found your way into me, feel an acute loss of an important part of myself as I struggle to drag my leg in before the door slides down. You are light on your feet, narrow as skis, and I am wide and corpulent, scared for the orderlies who will have to carryme when my joints dissolve completely. You wipe a leak from under my one eye, look straight at me. Say, *you ain't heavy, you're my lover.*

Kneeling

after *Kneeling Female Nude,* Unknown British Artist, Formerly Attributed to William Etty, after 1830

Penitence, patience, prayer, these things are empty around you. You beg for them but can't believe. Well, I was gone, too, for a long, long time, and I'm still not sure where to kneel. Say your grace the best way you know how, and know it is enough. There is a seat for you at the table, and a blessing in the cellar of salt. Mine was the small silver spoon; it flickered in flames from the candle, like somebody praying for me.

American Psycho

after *House by the Railroad,* Edward Hopper (USA) 1925

Another barren house at the top of a hill, another space emptied of spirit by the mother. She will find your skin and bones in the shower. She will be waiting for you at the foot of your bed. There is no sanctuary where the doors outside are always sealed, and the doors inside are never shut.

The Nowhere Train

after *The Chains That Free Us,* Cindy L. Sheppard (USA) 2017

Since we'd left the red hills behind, I couldn't shake the feeling that my newfound freedom was an illusion. I was thinking too much. Hurtling through those epic canyons had me reaching for more metaphors. No matter- there was no turning back. I had already decided to play the odds and take my chances.

I was tired of the crossword puzzle digest and my mystery novel. When the late light gave way to evening, I picked up some cards, started in on solitaire, and scrabbled through my duffel for my flask.

That's when the stranger appeared.

He pointed a chopstick finger at the seat across from me and I nodded. He was sharp and long and rubicund, like the red rock cliffs this afternoon. I retrieved my cards and Camels, made space for his strange narrow bones.

I'm too tired to sleep, he said, and gestured at my bottle. Do you mind? He reached for my cigarettes, then waited for a light. I couldn't read him at all, but I was sure he could read me.

We puffed and watched the darkness rolling past.

After a long while, he gathered up my deck and shuffled. I noticed then that the watch under his fraying cuffs was a classic Rolex. I was no expert on luxury bijouterie, but the diamante signet wobbling loosely to and fro on his pinkie also looked like the real deal.

He followed my eyes and I shifted uncomfortably. Crushed my smoke nervously in the window tray, lit another. The flask was still perched on the razor of his knee, but I knew it was nearing empty, so I waved an attendant down. Asked for a double Jack neat with ice on the side. I felt the stranger's small eyes drilling into me as he shuffled the cards methodically. Told the waiter to make it a round.

The stranger began doling out the cards. You can't always outrun someone's bluff, he said, and it sounded like a warning.

I'm running already, I wanted to say. I'm on my way there now, wherever it is. But I kept it to myself. I wondered how Adele would find me when she finally forgave me, since I didn't know myself where I was going.

We played a few hands, downed our liquor. I got a cold feeling way down deep when I caught the image of myself in the window. The stranger's reflection wasn't there.

Look, kiddo, my friend said, as suddenly as his glass was empty. The only way to win is to figure what you want to toss and what you want to save. It's not the hand you're dealt, but how you play it.

I was still mulling over everything in my mind, whether I should have cleaned up the mess I made with Adele before leaving, or boarded the train at all. Every cryptic thing the man said seemed to be on point. Even so, I resented the intrusion. I had wanted to wallow on my own, not waste my whiskey on unsolicited advice.

There was something creepy and familiar about him, too, almost like a déjà vu. And yet it felt in part as if he was a figment. As if he wasn't there all.

I threw down my turn, just passing the time, not really into the game. There was no expression on his face. The gambler's eyes in the night were twin beads, glittering only the reflection of my hand, deuce diamonds and hearts in spades.

Connective Tissue

after Fernando Botero

It's beautiful, really, my biology prof said, the collagen, the reticular fibres, the elasticity of it all, the patterns holding the adipose cells together. Like latticework, she told us. Beauty is not what I'm seeing now, in the Value Village lineup. Even with the six feet of separation, the old woman in front of me is like a cellulite scream, spilling out between fishnet diamonds and the armholes of a mesh tank shirt, hair bleached in bunches of orange and gray, with a vintage barrette that spells out "HOT" in garish rhinestones. She has yellow sneakers in her cart and a pile of leopard print garments. You almost *were* that lady in front of us, once, my sister says after we've paid and have left earshot. I feel a rush of relief for the office slacks and neat blazer in my bag, but it fades fast. Then it's me wondering what happened to me, wondering where it all went wrong.

The Skeleton Flower

after *Skeleton Flower,* Navaz DCruz, date and origin not known

He is telling us about the woman with a thousand umbrellas. How her halls are lined with a garden of brollies, chevron, checkers, damask and chintz. She disappears when the clouds come close, dissipating into vapor, into the thin air. She collects umbrellas to prevent her own vanishing. She is shy to shower in front of him, he says, turning to glass in the mist, invisible in mizzle. She is transparent when she cries. You can see right through her, like a window. It took some getting used to, he acknowledges, loving a girl who almost isn't there. Slippery when wet. She told him from the start the origin of her mystery- she was conceived in a grove of Diphylleia Grays. He explains: Diphylleia Grays are a woodland blossom, tiny and white. They transform to clear when watered, whether by hand or by dew. They look like crystal against the backdrop of leaves, so they are often called skeleton flowers. During the monsoons he grows lonely, he admits, but he is enchanted again and again by her strange and beautiful blooms. Look, he says, showing us a photograph of translucent efflorescence. See how her petals turn to rain.

Winter in June

after *Profile, Eye and Star,* Jean Cocteau (France) by 1963

He is talking about glaciers and the widest skies in the world, about a place called Gondwana that hasn't existed for two hundred million years. In June, the deep of winter, the moon is eternal and the sun does not rise. You imagine night horses with ice in their manes, galloping across snow-capped mountains. Where would you be if you weren't here? Maybe there, a little farther north, where Malbec flows from the limestone and men like this one dance the tango. You were too practical to run after him when you had the chance, didn't try to tame him into staying. You chose to set down roots, in the Northern hemisphere where the cold comes in January, without looking back. Found a man you can depend on, who still makes your heart race to this day, and you are happy. Still, as glasses clink and voices murmur, as guests choose carefully between Viognier and Pinot Noir, or Stilton and Gruyere, as your small audience takes in an arrangement of your pictures, you feel a strange sensation of thaw. It has been a few years since your southbound friend has made it home to one of your exhibitions; it has been nearly twenty since you slept together. Patrons are asking questions about your palette, about the meaning of the signs in your impasto. But you are somewhere else, just for the moment, in the crispy porch frost of a November dusk, melting, Coldplay on repeat, tumbling atop those so small hips, crushing them like winter birds.

"And the rest is rust and stardust."
Vladimir Nabakov

Acknowledgements

Thank you so much to all of the wonderful journals and small press literary publishers where these works first appeared.

Barn: Voice and Verse Literary Review
Benedict and the Pomelo: Flash Boulevard
Billy, Don't Lose My Number: MacQueen's Quinterly
Blindness: Cabinet of Heed
Blood: Litro Magazine
Boys of Summer: The Mantle
Bull: Flash Fiction North
Cages: Red Eft
Checkers: Indelible
The Chechia Makers: MacQueen's Quinterly
Cliff Hanger: City. River. Tree
Conceal/Carry: Flash Fiction North
Cuda: JMWW
Dandy Warhol: The Ekphrastic Review
Darker: Flash Boulevard
Day of the Dead: Eunoia Review
Death in Tepito: Rune Bear Weekly
Disco Nefertiti: Flash Fiction North
Downpour: Club Plum
Drowned World: Communicator's League
Eternity and Impermanence: The Ekphrastic World Anthology (The Ekphrastic Review)
Feeling the Blues: Halfway Down the Stairs
Fifteen Shades of Gray: Six Sentences
First Bluegrass Lesson: MacQueen's Quinterly

Found Objects: The Citron Review
The Garden: Rathalla Review
Girl at the Market: Indelible
Green Fan, Sleeping Lady: The Ekphrastic World Anthology (The Ekphrastic Review)
Hebe: The Ekphrastic World Anthology (The Ekphrastic Review)
The Hell Cat: The Plague Papers anthology, edited by Robbi Nester, Poemeleon
Homecoming: Voice and Verse Literary Review
Karen and Karen: Flash Fiction North
Kitten Heels: Hole in the Head Review
Kneeling: Six Sentences
Jalapeños: Art Ascent
The Keychain Monkeys: Flash Boulevard
The Last Time I Showed Up at Midnight: Bright Flash Literary Review
Lepidoptera: Cleaver Magazine
Lucky Peace: MacQueen's Quinterly
The Mists of Catalan: Hole in the Head Review
Mr. Jones: Flash Fiction North
Mrs. Jones: Flash Boulevard
The Neon Raven: MacQueen's Quinterly (first place winner in flash fiction contest)
Night Flight: Gyroscope Review
Night Swimming: Thimble
November Woods: Communicators League
The Nowhere Man: Communicators League
The Nowhere Train: South Florida Poetry Review
Online Quarantine Curiosity Cabinet, Amazon Edition: Pandemic Evolution: Poets Respond to the Art of Matthew Wolfe (anthology), Sheila Na Gig Editions, 2021

Our Daily Bread: Eunoia Review
Outlaw Shit: Fatal Flaw
The Paper Dark: Group of Seven Reimagined (anthology), edited by Karen Schauber, Heritage Books (This piece was nominated for the Pushcart Prize.)
A Parable of the Blind Leading the Blind: The Ekphrastic Review
The Peanut Butter Yarmulke: Flash Fiction North
Phantom of Flatwoods: MacQueen's Quinterly
Pho: MacQueen's Quinterly
The Pink Café: The Ekphrastic World Anthology (The Ekphrastic Review)
Promiscuity: MacQueen's Quinterly (This piece was nominated for the Pushcart Prize.)
Quill and Quire: Uppagus
Rapture: Flash Fiction North
The Red Van: South Shore Review
Robin Eggs: Indelible
Rocket Man: Visitant Lit
Ruby Slippers: Flash Fiction North
Running Hot and Cold: Floored (anthology) edited by Betsy Mars, Kingly Street Books
The Skeleton Flower: Unbroken Journal
Simon Says: Ghost Parachute (longlisted for the Furious Fiction Australia prize)
Soppressata: Brilliant Flash Fiction
Still Alive: Star 82
Stutter: Autumn Sky Poetry Daily
Sunday Bloody Sunday: The Plague Papers anthology, edited by Robbi Nester, Poemeleon
Sweet and Sour: Free Flash Fiction

Tightrope Love: Six Sentences
Tiny Dancer: Dropout Literary
Tower of Horses: The Ekphrastic Review
Twitter: MacQueen's Quinterly
Ventriloquy: Pandemic Evolution: Poets Respond to the Art of Matthew Wolfe (anthology), Sheila Na Gig Editions, 2021
white: The Ekphrastic Review
The White Room: Hole in the Head Review
Winter in June: Unbroken Journal
The Wishing Machine: Flash Boulevard
Yahtzee: Potato Soup Journal

Lorette C. Luzajic is an internationally collected visual artist, editor, educator, and writer. She studied journalism but prefers to write flash fiction and prose poetry. Her words have been widely published, nominated for the Pushcart Prize and Best of the Net, and translated into Urdu. Her lifelong passion is for art history. She is the founder and editor of *The Ekphrastic Review*, a journal devoted to literature inspired by visual art.

Selected Books by Lorette C. Luzajic

The Astronaut's Wife: poems of Eros and Thanatos
Solace
The Lords of George Street
Aspartame
Pretty Time Machine: ekphrastic prose poems
Salt: the essential poetry (Cyberwit Books)
Fascinating Writers: twenty-five unusual lives
Fascinating Artists: twenty-five unusual lives
Kilodney Does Shakespeare, and other stories
Truck, and other thoughts on art
Funny Stories About Depression

Made in the USA
Middletown, DE
01 July 2021